A PUFFIN BOOK

PROPERTY OF

_____

_____

SYLVIA WAUGH was born and brought up in Gateshead in the north-east of England. She was an English teacher for several years before becoming a full-time writer. In 1994 her debut novel, *The Mennyms*, won the *Guardian* Children's Fiction Prize, was shortlisted for the Carnegie Medal and received several other notable prizes, including the Birmingham Readers & Writers Children's Book Award. Sylvia continued the adventures of the life-sized family of rag dolls in four more Mennym books, all of which have been translated into many different languages. In 1997 she received the Dutch *Zilveren Zoen* (The Silver Kiss) Award for *The Mennyms* and in 2000 won the Austrian *Kinderbuchpreis* (Children's Book Prize) for the whole series. Her other published work includes the highly acclaimed Ormingat trilogy about an alien family sent to investigate life on Earth.

Sylvia still lives in Gateshead. She is married with three grown-up children and two nearly grown-up grandsons, and continues to write stories and poems for all ages.

Books by Sylvia Waugh

THE MENNYM SERIES

THE MENNYMS
MENNYMS IN THE WILDERNESS
MENNYMS UNDER SIEGE
MENNYMS ALONE
MENNYMS ALIVE

THE ORMINGAT TRILOGY

SPACE RACE
EARTHBORN
WHO GOES HOME?

SYLVIA WAUGH

The Mennyms

A PUFFIN BOOK

PUFFIN BOOKS

UK | USA | Canada | Ireland | Australia
India | New Zealand | South Africa

Puffin Books is part of the Penguin Random House group of companies
whose addresses can be found at global.penguinrandomhouse.com.

www.penguin.co.uk
www.puffin.co.uk
www.ladybird.co.uk

First published by Julia MacRae 1993
Published by Red Fox 1994
This edition published 2018

004

Text copyright © Sylvia Waugh, 1993

The moral right of the author has been asserted

Set in 12.5/16.5pt Sabon LT Std
Typeset by Jouve (UK), Milton Keynes
Printed and bound in Great Britain by Clays Ltd, Elcograf S.p.A.

A CIP catalogue record for this book is available from the British Library

ISBN: 978-0-241-34038-7

All correspondence to:
Puffin Books
Penguin Random House Children's
80 Strand, London WC2R ORL

MIX
Paper from
responsible sources
FSC® C018179

Penguin Random House is committed to a
sustainable future for our business, our readers
and our planet. This book is made from Forest
Stewardship Council® certified paper.

For my family

Contents

I, a stranger and afraid
In a world I never made.

Last Poems, A. E. Housman

1. The Letter

Loftus
Palmerston District
Dubbo
New South Wales
Australia
10th September

Dear Sir Magnus,

*Seems strange me writing a letter like this to a sir
and all that. I must admit I don't quite know how
to begin. You see, I've just inherited, among other
things, the house you have rented all these years
from my Uncle Chesney. Leastways, you did rent
from him till he died a few months back. Now it*

*appears that, as his sole kin, I am to become your
landlord.*

*Fancy me a landlord! And landlord to a real live
sir at that! If I sound a bit naive and over-
impressed, can't be helped. I am a fairly ordinary
bloke and I am impressed. I'm not a millionaire or
anything like that, but I'm a darn sight richer than I
was a while ago and I'm tickled pink to own a
property in England.*

*About me, since you must be wondering, I'm just
past thirty, unmarried (and with no intentions in
that direction) and I must've spent more time with
sheep than with people for the past ten year or
more. Now what with the land here I've been left,
and a tidy bit of money, I'm thinking of coming, for
the first time ever, to the old country to see a bit of
the world and, if you've got no objection, to pay
you a visit. Not as a landlord lording it, you know,
but, I hope, as a friend to you and your family.*

*From what I can gather, you've been tenants at
Brocklehurst Grove since old Auntie Kate died nigh
on forty year ago. Uncle Ches was a wee bit vague
about how you come to take over, but then Uncle
Ches was vague about most things. Except money!
I see you paid his agents the rent, and a fair rent at
that. He had no cause to grumble. Still, you never*

*did get to meet him, so I won't speak no ill of
the dead.*

*I suppose you must be getting on a bit by now.
Forty is a considerable number of years. I hope this
letter finds you a hale and hearty granpa! I
understand from the papers the agents hold that
you are blessed with a wife and family. Tulip struck
me as a curious name for a woman, but real pretty
when you come to think of it. I hope that you and
all of yours are thriving.*

*It's my purpose to come your side late
November. I don't want to intrude at all, but I'd
love to meet all of you and see the house where
Great Aunt Kate was born and lived out all her
days. Uncle Ches used to shake his head and say she
was a 'character', but he never did specify how.*

*I look forward to enjoying your company and
hearing all your memories. I hope you will look on
me as part of your family. I have no other family of
my own.*

*Yours very sincerely,
Albert Pond*

2. Consternation

THE LETTER from Albert Pond shot through the tightly sprung letter-box of 5 Brocklehurst Grove on a wet October morning before any of its residents had stirred from their beds. It was Saturday.

'Sounds like the postman's been,' said Vinetta with a yawn. Joshua turned in his sleep and grunted. He didn't want to wake up. His tattered left leg was wrapped to the knee in an old bath towel and he was not looking forward to the day ahead.

'I suppose I'd better go and look,' said Vinetta, pulling herself up out of bed and putting on her slippers. The curtains showed a pale daylight. So she went downstairs without switching on the light and picked up the airmail letter from the doormat.

An airmail letter, she thought with some surprise. The only letters the Mennyms ever received were of the business sort: cheques for Sir Magnus and other letters from his publishers, household bills and receipts, catalogues for Appleby, and occasional flattering offers to take part in prize draws. Never personal letters. And never, never letters from abroad.

Vinetta looked at the envelope more carefully. 'It's for Granpa!' she exclaimed.

In the best bedroom at the front of the house, Granpa Mennym was still asleep. His elegant white moustache flowed over his lips. He had been born knowing a thousand pearls of wisdom. That is a lot of knowledge. So he found it necessary to lie and think deep thoughts every day of his life. His advice was not always taken, but it was deemed to be well worth hearing.

Magnus was, physically, the least active member of the family. He never left his bed. His only mobility was in one purple velvet foot that dangled from the counterpane. The twins, Poopie and Wimpey, sometimes tried to rouse their grandfather by swinging on this tempting appendage, but soon the foot would simply grow forcefully rigid and kick the two of them to the other side of the room. Then they would scream the place down as if the impact had really hurt them. It was one of their favourite pretends.

If their mother, Vinetta, was by when this happened, she would say briskly, 'Don't make such a fuss, you two. It'd take more than Granpa's foot to knock the stuffing out of you. Go and play with Googles. Or ask Appleby to show you her stamp collection.'

When Vinetta came to Granpa's room on this particular October morning, the old man did not stir. The purple foot dangled limply over the edge of the bed.

'Granpa,' said Vinetta loudly as she opened the curtains, 'there's a letter for you from Australia. Isn't that where the owner lives?'

Granpa looked at her sharply, focusing the black button eyes that never closed in sleep, but could vary from the dull opaque of dreaming to the bright gleam of intelligent thought.

'Yes, it is,' he growled, not at all pleased at being aroused from his slumbers. 'Wonder what he wants. In forty years we've never heard directly from him before. She's paid the rent, hasn't she?'

'Of course she has,' said Vinetta indignantly. 'Besides, it might not be from him.'

'And who else in Australia would have heard of us?' Sir Magnus gave his daughter-in-law a withering look.

From the dressing room next door, Granny Tulip called plaintively, 'What is it? What is it now?' She had chosen to sleep in the small room because she was often wakeful at night and liked to get on with her knitting, sometimes in the wee small hours. She was ceaselessly active. All day she would sit in the breakfast room downstairs knitting garments for the whole family. Her needles moved with fascinating speed. All of her movements were quick and economical. Even her speech was rapid and purposeful.

Within seconds she was at Grandpa's bedside. She was, as always, fully dressed, wearing a blue and white checked apron. She was a very neat little woman with pure white hair and a deceptively tolerant, friendly expression on her fine-featured face. Without a word, she took the envelope from Granpa's large mittened fingers and deftly opened it. Taking care of the bills was, after all, her job. And, until the letter was opened, who was to say that it was not some unusual demand for money?

What she read, through her little round spectacles, made her gasp in surprise.

'Well I never,' she huffed and read on as the other two watched her with keen curiosity.

'Just imagine!' she exclaimed.

'Fancy that!' she muttered as she reached the end of the second page.

'What is it, Gran?' demanded Vinetta at last.

'He's coming here. He's coming next month to see us all!'

A dull horror came over the room.

'He can't be,' bellowed Magnus forcibly, speaking from the depths of his great knowledge and his mound of snowy white pillows. 'He must be about eighty by now. He won't be gallivanting all the way from Australia to see us after all these years. He didn't bother when he was forty. He certainly won't bother at eighty. You haven't read the letter properly, woman.'

'Don't you woman me!' snapped Granny Tulip. 'I've read it all right. It's not Chesney who's coming. It's his nephew. Chesney's dead. The new owner is called Albert Pond. This could be serious.'

'He owns the house now,' said Vinetta doubtfully.

Magnus looked at the two women bleakly, his black eyes turning dull and lifeless.

'Yes,' he said in a grim voice, 'if that's the case. He owns the house. It could fairly be argued that he owns us too.'

'We pay the rent,' said Tulip firmly. 'Every month on the dot I send a cheque to the agents. There can't be a better payer than us. Whenever they have increased the payment, we have paid the extra without a murmur. And we haven't asked for any repairs to be done. We are ideal tenants. The new owner should be satisfied with that.'

'If he ever finds out what we really are,' groaned Granpa, 'I shudder to think what he might do.' So saying, he turned his back on the two women and pulled the counterpane right over his head.

3. The Problem

BROCKLEHURST Grove was built round three sides of a large square. The fourth side was the main road passing through the town. It was ideally situated, just five minutes' walk from the shops on the High Street, but looking as if it belonged to a country village. The statue of Matthew James Brocklehurst, standing on its tiered pedestal in the centre of the square, looked comfortably provincial.

The houses were at the upper end of the suburban market, large, detached and with very private, well-hedged gardens. Numbers 1 to 3 were on the left-hand side, numbers 7 to 9 were on the right. At the back, furthest from the main road, were numbers 4 to 6 and, naturally, number 5, where the Mennyms lived, was exactly in the centre.

The family at number 5 were not well-known. They were not invisible, but they preferred not to be noticed and, on the whole, nobody noticed them. Mr and Mrs Jarman, who had lived for twenty-five years at number 4, were very friendly with the Englands who now lived at number 6. They'd only moved in four years before, but they had struck up a friendship immediately. Some people are like that. Not the Mennyms. No one in the street had ever passed the time of day with any of the residents of number 5.

The Mennyms, it must be said, had good reason to hold themselves aloof. It was not that they felt superior, having lived there far longer than anybody else. With the exception of Miss Quigley, they would hardly have known what feeling superior or inferior meant. It was simply that they would not dare to mix with outsiders.

They were not human, you see – at least not in the normal sense of the word. They were not made of flesh and blood. They were just a whole, lovely family of life-size rag dolls. They were living and walking and talking and breathing, but they were made of cloth and kapok. They each had a little voice box, like the sort they put in teddy bears to make them growl realistically. Their frameworks were strong but pliable. Their respiration kept their bodies supplied with oxygen that was life to the kapok and sound to the voices.

Their maker was an extremely gifted seamstress called Kate Penshaw. She never knew why she made them. It was just a rather unusual hobby pursued obsessively by a lonely old lady. She never even noticed the life lying dormant in their huge cloth bodies. It was only after she died and was buried that her creations came out of their silence and methodically took over the house.

Technically the property belonged to a nephew called Chesney Loftus who lived in Australia, but he had never returned to claim it.

There were no complaints about the house being neglected and unlived in. Vinetta kept the windows clean and washed the net curtains. Joshua and the twins took care of the garden. Poopie, in fact, had proved to be quite skilled in looking after the plants. In a variety of ways, they managed to make enough money to pay the bills, and to buy this and that from time to time.

Being rag dolls, they did not need any food. They did use heating to keep warm and dry. They found that they could see with their bright button eyes. Their felt ears proved successful at hearing and their mouths learned to open and shape words. Their brains, made of kapok, were no worse, and in some cases much better, than many of the human variety.

The Mennyms had very soon realised that they would need a policy for survival in an alien world. Their first law was to have as little contact as possible with human beings. No outsider must ever notice that they were not made of flesh and blood. When they went out, they hurried there and back, hidden in clothing and wearing brimmed hats or, if the weather permitted, carrying a large umbrella.

They learned how to use the telephone. They managed to open a bank account without actually going into a bank. It was perfectly possible in those days. They even rummaged through Kate's old desk and discovered an agent to whom they could pay the rent. That had involved some deception, but Appleby Mennym proved very adept at inventing explanations whenever they were required. Chesney Loftus, indirectly, was informed of the names of his aunt's 'paying guests' and of their request to remain on as tenants in the property. This was all done very legally, with both Sir Magnus and his son Joshua signing the tenancy agreement. The agreement was very much in favour of the owner, freeing him from all responsibility for the upkeep of the property and ensuring him a regular income from a monthly rent that could be increased if its real value dropped. The phrase 'in line with inflation' was not in use at the time, but that was what was meant. The annual increase was sometimes a little on the high side, but the Mennyms were able to pay and were, in any case, in no position to argue.

Kate, maybe accidentally, had left them well provided for. In her huge work-box, which looked more like a wicker trunk, she had left a cache of money which was sufficient to provide for the Mennyms in the difficult period of transition between her death and their life.

All that was very long ago. The Mennyms, over the years, had become a successful family unit, able to cope with almost anything.

They played at living and developed talents. Sir Magnus lay on his bed and, for two hours every day, including Sundays, he wrote interesting articles which he sold, by post, to various newspapers and periodicals. Appleby used to go to the Post Office, in disguises that matched the time of year, and buy stamps or hand over the letters without ever raising her head.

Joshua made a small but steady income in the various jobs he managed to do without being observed. It was quite difficult for him since he was nowhere near as clever as his father. Vinetta had learned how to sew, at first using Kate's old treadle sewing machine. Over the years she had progressed to more modern machines, but she still used the old one from time to time, especially if she was worried about anything.

As for the children, they had lessons from Tulip and Vinetta on a regular basis and were occasionally tutored by Sir Magnus. Appleby was his favourite pupil. She flattered him quite blatantly and pretended to be interested in everything. He would smile at her indulgently and enquire about her pocket money which she would reluctantly admit was never plentiful enough to buy all the things she needed. Then a helpful hand would reach under the pillow and draw out a leather pouch from which he would take a few coins to hand over slyly.

'Say nothing to the others,' he would whisper. 'You're a good lass. You deserve a little extra.'

Soobie, the blue Mennym, had read every book in the house at least twice. No one could teach him anything and he was not willing to play at lessons as the others were. He would sometimes ask his grandfather searching questions to which the old man, clever though he was, did not always know the answers.

Poopie was more like Joshua, good at practical things. As for Wimpey, she was a wide-eyed dreamer with long golden ringlets. She believed in fairy tales and was always waiting for something magical to happen. Little Googles gurgled in her cot or her pram and was regularly, though unnecessarily, 'changed and fed'.

Miss Quigley led the narrowest life, dull and undeveloped, but that was because she was just a visitor and spent most of her time in the hall cupboard.

They lived cheaply, of course. They did not eat or drink except as a glorious pretend. And they never went on holiday, though they liked to read the brochures.

Naturally, they never grew any older. Googles had been a baby for forty years. Sir Magnus was seventy when he was first made and was still seventy when the letter from Australia fell through the letter-box.

All that enchanted world was now in peril.

For forty years they had come and gone surreptitiously in the neighbourhood, even managing to shop without being noticed. But, as Sir Magnus proclaimed when next they consulted him, you cannot sit in the same room as a man without observing that he is flesh and blood. He, in turn, would look across the table at a cloth face with button eyes and would be horrified.

'Not horrified!' exclaimed Vinetta as she sat by her father-in-law's bed. 'We may be strange. I know we are strange. But surely we are not horrific? At a distance we look just like anybody else.'

'To him we would be horrific,' insisted Sir Magnus, his moustache twitching knowingly. 'At least at first we would be. If he proved to be unscrupulous, he could come round to seeing us as valuable curiosities, and that would be worse.'

'We are not valuable! Even my wedding ring is made of brass!' Vinetta looked down at her plain cotton skirt, neatly patched in places.

'Any curiosity can have its value,' declared Sir Magnus pompously. He propped himself up higher against the mound of pillows and placed his hand over Vinetta's. 'I don't think you realise how unique we are. But you have watched television. You must have realised that man-sized, talking, rational rag dolls do not exist anywhere else in the world.'

Vinetta thought briefly of the Muppets, but appreciated the difference even as she thought.

'What is unique and curious must be very valuable,' pronounced Sir Magnus. He then sank down into his pillows, a gesture of dismissal. Vinetta rose and, carrying away the dreadful letter, left Granpa to his thoughts.

4. The Rat

THE MENNYMS had problems enough already that day without the dire news from across the world. There was Joshua's foot, for a start, and all the complications that involved.

For the past five years or more, Joshua had been nightwatchman at Sydenham's Electrical Warehouse on the other side of town. He always walked there, quickly, well-muffled, with his head down and his whole body bent forcefully forward.

The interview for this job had taken place on a freezing cold Friday afternoon in a badly-lit and unheated gatehouse. His employer had barely looked at him. Joshua remembered the bald patch in the middle of the man's head as he bent over the desk where a little pool of light shone on the letter of application Appleby had written. Joshua's cap had been well down over his brows. The collar of his thick overcoat had been turned up round his ears. He needn't have worried, though. Clarence Sydenham had just mumbled on about the duties and the wages and then thrust a paper at him for his signature. Joshua had gripped the pen in his gloved hand and scribbled his name as quickly as he could. Clarence had switched off the table-lamp and hurried out to make his getaway in his Ford Transit.

At the time, Joshua had been delighted. Interviews were always a gamble. There had been times when he had seen that the risk was too great and he had turned away from premises much more inviting to mortal men but far too public for rag dolls.

The job was not well paid, but it was adequate and it had many compensations in Joshua's eyes. He would sit all night in the little office, taking a walk round the aisles of shelves once an hour or so. Then he would be ready at seven sharp, head down in the hood of his duffle coat, to mutter good morning to Charlie, who always arrived first, and to hand over the keys to him.

'Quiet night?' Charlie would enquire in a routine way, as he went to hang his coat on the coat stand in the corner of the office.

'Very quiet,' Joshua would reply to the back of Charlie's head. Then he would hurry out as if to catch a bus. But he didn't. He hastened, head down but watchful, along three miles of streets to his home. Public transport was too well lit and too confined for him to dare to use it.

All was well till the Thursday before Albert Pond's letter arrived. On that Thursday night Joshua had been at work as usual. He had done several 'prowls' to make sure that there were no intruders. (There never were. His movements round the building and the lights he switched on and off at irregular intervals must have been a sufficient deterrent.) An automatic alarm system had recently been installed but Joshua always turned it off as soon as he came in. Newfangled, unnecessary thing!

He had read the evening paper. He had even clasped his hands round a mug of cocoa and made believe he was drinking it. Not that there was anyone there to see him, but he liked the pretend. It relieved the monotony.

Then he settled back in his chair for a little snooze. It was a nice old office, very functional; a couple of metal filing cabinets, a strong desk, a dim ceiling light with a white enamel shade, a thin carpet not quite covering all the floorboards, and with a that-could-trip-anybody-up frayed patch in front of the gas fire. Not a bad job, all considered.

Then suddenly, as Joshua slept, disaster struck.

Through the part-open glass door from the warehouse floor came a large and hungry rat. The metal boxes on the warehouse shelves had offered no sustenance. The rat sniffed round cautiously. Then he came under the old kneehole desk to Joshua's boot. Placidly but industriously, he began to gnaw at it. Then, finding the leather none too juicy but feeling confident that no human being was about to attack him, the rat crawled further up Joshua's leg and ate right through his trousers till bits of kapok began to flutter to the floor.

Joshua awoke from his catnap and hearing scuffling around his knee looked down and was horrified. As soon as he jumped up, the rat dived out into the darkness.

But it was too late. The damage had been done.

Rag dolls feel no pain. The wound, if you could call it that, did not hurt him. But he was, after all, a living being. Pain is of the flesh, but fear is of the mind. Joshua looked at his tattered knee and was terrified.

The clock on the wall said twenty to six. Joshua had just an hour and twenty minutes to get ready. It was not going to be easy, not one little bit. He looked hard at the knee with the stuffing falling out and at the gnawed boot below it. Easy? It might not even be possible. Ten of his precious minutes were spent in paralysed fright. He had sat down heavily as soon as the rat fled. Now he didn't know whether he would be able to rise again, let alone walk.

'I'll have to do something,' he said to himself at last. The first thing was to stop any more stuffing from falling out and to push back as much as he could. Opening the desk drawer he found, to his relief, a roll of sticky tape. Another drawer obligingly supplied a pair of scissors. So, with as much skill as he could muster, he began to carry out an emergency repair. He wished Vinetta were there. She was much better at that sort of thing.

After a great struggle, the leg had at least stopped shedding any more stuffing. It looked abnormal and ugly with the trouser leg hanging raggedly round it. But all that could be hidden by his duffle coat. The problem now was to find out if the leg could still manage to support his weight and to walk in a reasonable manner.

Joshua stood up. That was all right. He held the desk with both hands and gingerly moved his good foot one step back. Then he tried to do the same with his bad foot. But instead of obediently joining its partner the silly thing went off to one side. Joshua looked down at it unbelievingly. He knew where he had told the foot to go and it hadn't gone there. With regard to standing, it made little difference. He still had both hands on the desk and his feet, instead of being together, were spread astride.

He looked sternly at his disobedient left limb and willed it to work its way towards its partner. That worked. He gave a half-hearted sigh of relief.

Taking his hands from the desk, he stood upright and made a determined effort to reach the coat stand. The result was what can only be described as a 'funny-walk' in classic funny-walk style. The right foot trod firmly. The left one shot out in front before crashing down on a place on the floor about six inches ahead of where it should have been. This set the right foot slightly off balance but, being a clever and orderly right foot, it soon learned to correct its mate's eccentricity.

I suppose I'll manage, thought Joshua bleakly, but it'll be a slow job.

He looked at the clock and saw that it was twenty-five to seven. Quickly he put his coat on and went and stood in the doorway to wait for Charlie.

It was a cold morning. So it didn't look too odd that Joshua was muffled up in his hood and that one of Tulip's scarves was wrapped right round his chin.

'You're in a hurry this morning, old man,' chaffed Charlie as Joshua hastily handed over the keys before the newcomer had even crossed the doorstep.

'Full of cold,' sniffed Joshua. 'Be glad to get home to bed.'

Charlie went in to hang his coat up and Joshua took that opportunity to get his funny-walk round the corner out of sight. Charlie turned round to make some other friendly remark and shrugged when he saw that the nightwatchman was already gone.

'Odd bloke,' he said to himself. 'Seen him five mornings a week for years. Yet I don't really know anything about him, or, for that matter, even what he looks like under all that clobber.'

Meantime, Joshua was off with his funny-walk down the quiet back lanes and side streets on a journey that took him twice as long as usual and got more and more difficult as he drew near his home. People looked askance at him. The walk was by no means unobtrusive. Fortunately, the bulky figure in the big duffle coat did not look approachable. And equally fortunately, it was still a little too early for the children to be going to school. A paperboy did shout after him, 'You'll never get to play for Accrington Stanley, mister.' Apart from that he was unmolested.

When he got to Brocklehurst Grove, he became more worried. It must have been about eight-thirty. He saw from the corner a car gliding out of the drive at number 1. After it passed, he walked cautiously by the high hedge, brushing the twigs with his shoulder, trying desperately hard to be invisible.

At number 2 all of the curtains were still closed and the door looked firmly shut.

Number 3 was the worst. Four snooty children in assorted school uniforms were scrambling noisily into the family car.

'At least I've done my homework,' shrieked one of them in a voice that carried to the street. 'I'm not a lazy beggar like you.'

'Get in,' said their father, 'and shut up.'

Car doors slammed.

Joshua froze. Any minute the car with its menagerie would swing out into the street. It would pass close to him. Those awful children would see his funny-walk and jeer. And he couldn't just stand still. That would look suspicious.

In an agony of suspense, he gingerly bent his good leg and spent what seemed like forever unfastening and then carefully refastening his boot lace.

The car passed by.

Joshua stood up ready to walk on, but the left leg shot forward before the right one was properly balanced. Down he fell on his bottom on the pavement, his mittened hands shooting behind him to stop him falling further. Two of the children in the back of the car saw this and pointed and giggled. But the car with the objectionable youngsters was soon out of sight.

From behind the net curtains in her front bedroom window, Mrs Jarman at number 4 saw Joshua fall. She knew him vaguely by sight, the shape of him anyway. If he had not got straight up she would have gone down to see if he needed help. As he disappeared behind her hedge, she had a glimpse of the funny-walk, but put it down to awkwardness after his fall and thought no more about it. The Mennyms were known to keep themselves to themselves. Well, let them.

Vinetta was already at the front door looking out for him. When she saw his funny-walk coming up the drive, she pursed her lips in annoyance.

'What do you think you are playing at? Do you want everyone looking at you?' she snapped. 'Where on earth have you been all this time?'

As he drew closer and she saw the misery on his face, she realised that something was really wrong. She ran to him and supported him on her shoulder into the house.

5. The Leg

WHEN Vinetta saw Joshua's leg and heard
the tale he had to tell, she was all concern
and sympathy. She had never seen a rat except in
Aunt Kate's encyclopaedia. But she knew she
would have been ten times as terrified as Joshua if
the same thing had happened to her.

'You were very brave,' she said soothingly. At
the same time she looked at the damaged leg and
thought silently that he had made a very poor job
of taping it up. A neater job would have been
more easily undone. As it was, the leg from the
thigh nearly to the top of his boot was swathed in
crumpled sticky tape. Obviously done in a panic.
Removing it would not be pleasant.

Staying matter-of-fact, Vinetta helped Joshua to his usual armchair and turned on the television where the morning news was slowing down to a trickle. She gave him a pretend mug of tea and he went through the usual, reassuring ritual of make-believe drinking.

'That was nice. You do make a good cup of tea,' he said as he put the mug down on the little table by the side of his chair. Vinetta could make everything seem manageable and normal. As the news finished, she turned off the TV.

'Now,' said Vinetta cautiously, 'I will have to do something about that leg.'

Joshua looked as if he had much rather not, but he knew that he would have to accept the inevitable.

'First I'll remove all of that sticky tape,' said Vinetta firmly. She tugged at it ruthlessly till tape and kapok and bits of leg were strewn all round his feet. Joshua watched in dazed dismay.

Ignoring the expression on her husband's face, Vinetta said in her most businesslike manner, 'I'll have to go to the Market and get a length of material and some filling to renew that leg.'

It was easy to shop in the Market with a hat or headscarf pulled well over one's face, a pair of tinted spectacles to hide the button eyes and a coat collar turned up to give more shadow. Vinetta often went to the Market. But Market days were Thursday and Saturday. Joshua knew that well enough.

'What about work tonight? I'll need my leg before then.'

'Can't be done,' said Vinetta. 'You'll just have to be off sick. That's something you haven't done before. You are within your rights.'

Joshua looked unconvinced. In fact, he looked positively worried.

'I don't know how to be off sick. Somebody would have to be told. That firm trusts me.'

'Phone them,' said Vinetta practically, 'or let me phone them for you.'

Joshua's expression became pained.

'Apart from that first interview, which was mercifully short, I've never spoken to them. I don't want to speak to them. They might get friendly. They might send Charlie round to see how I am. It's too involved. It's dangerous.'

Vinetta could see the point of this.

'We'll ask Appleby,' she said at last. It wasn't that Appleby was wiser than anybody else. It was just that the whole family knew, as after forty years of living together they were bound to know, that their adolescent member was better than any of them at creating plausible fictions.

'Appleby,' called her mother from the foot of the stairs. 'Appleby!'

Vinetta's voice rose an octave and sounded irritated.

'What do you want now?' snapped her gangly daughter, leaning over the banister.

'Is that any way to speak to your mother?' said Vinetta crossly. 'You're getting worse. I wouldn't have called you so early if it weren't important. Come down here and I'll explain.'

Appleby came slowly down the stairs. She was a long, thin girl doll dressed in jeans and a very long, narrow sweater (not made by Kate or Vinetta, but bought quite recently at the Market).

'Well?' she pouted. Kate had somehow put truculence into Appleby's soul. It took different forms at different times, but it was always there. She was nearest in age to Soobie, but they were so totally unalike that it was difficult to see them as members of the same family. Her face for a start was flesh pink and Soobie's, unique even in this odd family, was completely blue. It was stocky, sturdy Soobie, with his silver button eyes and suit of striped blue linen, who sat quietly, day in day out, at the bay window watching the birds and the trees and the people who passed by their wrought-iron gate. Soobie never went out at all. He would watch Appleby as she came and went to the Market or the Post Office. Appleby was always coming or going somewhere, once the streets had been aired. She had never in forty years seen the dawn of any day.

'Try to be a bit more civil,' complained Vinetta, knowing that the appeal would fall on deaf ears. Appleby clattered down the stairs and dropped to the floor in front of the fire. If the state of her father's leg puzzled her she managed not to show it.

Vinetta explained the problem. Appleby's manner changed at once. When her special skills were called into play, nobody could be nicer.

'They must have word today,' she said decisively. 'They'll be livid if the warehouse is left unattended tonight. I don't know what's so wrong about phoning.'

'I'm not phoning,' interrupted Joshua in a determined voice.

'All right! All right! Nobody said you had to phone!'

'And you're not phoning either. Nobody's speaking to anybody there. Understood?'

'Well, if you would shut up for a minute, I can tell you what we should do,' said Appleby, becoming disagreeable again. She stood up and flounced over to the chair by the window, passing Soobie on the way and accidentally-on-purpose knocking his book out of his hand.

'Give over,' growled Soobie, retrieving the book and returning to his reading without another word.

'All right,' said Vinetta patiently. 'We're listening, Appleby. What do you think should be done?'

Appleby gave her father a token dirty look and decided to return to the topic more graciously.

'Simple. I'll write you a note and Mum can hand it in at the gatehouse and hurry away.'

The note was written as if it came from Vinetta.

'Dear Sir,' it began.

'Do we need to say dear anything?' grumbled Joshua. 'I'm just the nightwatchman, you know. There's nobody there I'd call dear. Or sir for that matter.'

'It's the way it's done, Dad,' explained Appleby with some irritation. 'Ask Granpa. He knows. I don't know why you two know nothing.'

Vinetta gave her daughter a sharp look but did not speak.

Appleby read out the whole of the note in clipped tones and double-quick time:

'Dear Sir,

My husband will not be able to come to work for a few days. He has a very heavy cold and is running a temperature.

By the way, he says he saw a rat in the warehouse last night. He thinks you should get the ratcatcher before any damage is done to the stores.

Yours sincerely,
Vinetta Mennym'

'Why mention the rat?' demanded Joshua crossly.

'You do want to go back there, don't you?'

'Of course I do. It's my job. It helps pay the bills.'

'Well, you don't want any more trouble with rats when you do go back. It's a pity really that you can't claim compensation.'

'Don't be so stupid,' shouted Joshua. 'You're supposed to know so much, Miss Bighead. How would I explain about the stuffing in my leg without giving everything away? Tell me that!'

At that moment, because he was agitated, more of the kapok fell to the floor.

'I'll have to do a temporary repair on that,' said Vinetta. She returned in a few minutes carrying a woolly hat and a big old bath towel.

'See,' she said matching actions to words, 'I'll pad the hole out with this old hat and then I'll wrap the towel round your leg and fasten it with four safety pins. It can stay like that till I've been to the Market.'

After she had finished she helped Joshua up to bed and told him firmly that he must stay there all day and all night.

'Appleby can take the note along to Sydenham's and she'll get you a newspaper on her way back.'

Appleby, however, had exhausted herself writing the letter.

'I'm not going out this morning. In fact, I might not go out at all today. Why should I run about after everybody? You got me up too soon. I'm tired.'

It was easy for Appleby to go anywhere. If there were any chance that she might be looked at too closely, she wore a black felt hat with a floppy brim that hid most of her doll's face. She had also taken in recent months to wearing rather exaggerated makeup. In fact, green button eyes apart, she looked like any other teenager.

Vinetta was used to Appleby's rudeness. She had suffered it in various forms for forty years. If the current phase seemed even worse than all the others put together, Vinetta could only wait and hope it would pass.

So she did not insist or argue. She simply said in an acid voice, 'If it is so much trouble to you, I'll do it myself. Mind you, I won't be in a hurry the next time you want something stitched or washed at short notice.'

6. Redundant

Dear Mr Mennym,

Thank you for your note explaining your unavoidable absence. This letter is in no way connected with your illness. We have been well satisfied with your timekeeping and attention to duty and will be pleased to recommend you to any future employer.

It has, however, been pointed out to us that, since the installation of the new security system four months ago, the position of nightwatchman is now redundant. You have seen the system through its early teething troubles and we express our sincere appreciation of your work. Your information about the rat was dealt with on Friday afternoon. It turned out to be just one stray animal that had come

*up from a drain at the back of our premises where
the Gas Board workmen have been digging.*

*The enclosed cheque is to cover payment in lieu
of notice, redundancy money and a gratuity for your
promptness in spotting and reporting the vermin
problem.*

*Please accept our best wishes for a speedy
recovery and a prosperous future.*

*Yours most sincerely,
Clarence & Joseph Sydenham*

Joshua let the cheque flutter to the floor and
almost wept as he read the letter. He had enjoyed
being nightwatchman at Sydenham's; it had
become an important part of his life. It was not a
well-paid job. Sir Magnus made far more money
with his writing. Vinetta's needlework also paid
well. No one ever knew how much Tulip earned.
But Joshua liked to feel he was doing his share.
Even rag dolls have bills to pay and things they
want to buy.

The leg was completely whole again and he had
a new pair of trousers which Vinetta had bought
from a stall in the Market and altered to fit her
husband's shape and size. He really looked quite

smart. And Charlie would never have a glimpse of the new trousers! And the warehouse keys would never be in Joshua's hands again.

'I've left my mug there,' he said at last. 'I've a good mind to go and fetch it.'

'That would be just plain stupid,' said Vinetta. 'You couldn't just walk in and grab it. Their security system would see to that. And what's so special about a mug anyway?'

'It was mine,' said Joshua with unusual feeling. 'It had a shield painted on it with the words "Port Vale F.C. – 1876" wrapped round. I used to put hot water in it and hold it cupped in my hands on a cold night and pretend it was cocoa and I was drinking it. I love that mug, Vinetta.'

'There are other mugs,' said Vinetta, deliberately missing the point, 'and there'll be other jobs. Why not go back to Peachum's and see if they'll have you as Santa Claus again?'

'That won't be for at least another four weeks,' grumbled Joshua. 'What'll I do in the meantime? I'm a working man and I want to work.'

'Well, let's pretend you need a few weeks to get fit. After all, you did have a very bad leg. If you had been flesh and blood you might never have walked again.'

'If I'd been flesh and blood, the rat would never have dared do what it did. Talk sense, woman!'

Vinetta persisted. She was used to persisting. After forty years it had become second nature.

'Never mind that,' she went on. 'Just let's pretend you really are a bit ill, and I can give you make-believe medicine, and you can sit all day in your dressing-gown and carpet slippers reading the papers and watching the telly.'

That sounded quite interesting. Joshua perked up and joined in the new pretend with growing enthusiasm.

'Then I'll gradually get a little bit better,' he said, 'and I'll take short walks round the block, well wrapped up against the frosty weather. Mother can knit me a new pair of gloves. Green ones.'

At that moment Poopie came running into the room followed by Wimpey who was shouting, 'Give me my ribbon back or I'll never play with you again.'

'Stop that, you two,' said their mother firmly. 'Your father is not at all well. He needs peace and quiet.'

Soobie looked curiously from his armchair in the bay window. The blue Mennym was the least given to pretending. He was usually satisfied just to sit and watch, but occasionally the family craze for pretends got on his nerves.

By the time Appleby came down for her make-believe breakfast, the latest pretend was well established. She was told all about it and she entered into the spirit of it with great gusto.

'I can go to the chemist and buy some proper medicine,' she suggested. 'That would make it seem more real.'

'What sort of medicine?' demanded Joshua doubtfully.

'The cheapest I can get, of course,' said Appleby. 'After all, it's really just the bottle and the spoon we are interested in.'

Soobie groaned. It wouldn't have been so bad, he thought, if they had all been mad enough to believe in their own play-acting. But there they were, fully accepting that it was all made up, and yet going through with it as if it were necessary.

The mention of a bottle reminded Vinetta that it must be feeding and changing time for Googles. She hurried into the little side room where the baby was gurgling in her cot. With loving care Vinetta changed her unsoiled nappy, then went to the kitchen to fetch the bottle that was standing ready, warming in a pan full of hot water.

'Bye Baby Bunting,' she sang. 'Your daddy's gone a-hunting . . .'

Wimpey had followed her mother into the room and was sitting at her feet.

'Our daddy can't go anywhere,' she said sagely. 'He's not at all well, Googles. He needs peace and quiet.'

7. A Visit from Miss Quigley

ON TUESDAY afternoon at ten to two, the door to the hall cupboard was opened from the inside. Vinetta, who was hanging the family's outdoor coats up on the rack in the hall (no one else in the family could be persuaded to be so tidy), politely turned the other way.

The twins, Poopie and Wimpey, were in the playroom playing Monopoly rather noisily. Soobie was at his window in the lounge. They did not hear the cupboard door open.

Joshua, in the kitchen, still in dressing-gown and slippers, was pretending to make a pot of tea in Aunt Kate's old brown teapot. He heard the door open, raised his woolly eyebrows, but did not look round from his task.

Appleby alone, coming down the stairs at that precise moment, saw the door open and spitefully stared at it as Miss Quigley emerged. Miss Quigley became aware of her staring and felt quite flustered and embarrassed. The feeling conveyed itself to Vinetta.

'I wish you would learn to hang your coat up, Appleby,' snapped Vinetta. 'I don't know how many times I have to tell you. The hall table is not the place to put it. We might be having visitors this afternoon for all you know.'

Miss Quigley, in her neat brown tweed suit with brown gloves and shoes and carrying a large brown handbag, slipped gratefully into the kitchen whilst Appleby's attention was distracted.

In the kitchen, Joshua was pouring imaginary tea into a large, old, slightly chipped cup. He ignored Miss Quigley as she passed him to leave the house by the back door. That was the way it worked, the way it had always worked for forty long years. No one ever spoke to Miss Quigley on her way out to the back. They did not want to embarrass her by making her aware that she just lived in a cupboard and did not really have a small house of her own at the end of Trevethick Street.

The back door closed behind her and Joshua put his cup down and went out into the hall.

'I think I ought to get dressed,' he said grumpily to Vinetta who by now had started polishing the hall table. 'We might have company this afternoon. I would feel very stupid going round like this.'

Vinetta looked annoyed.

'I thought we had decided you could be ill for three weeks. Tulip hasn't finished knitting your gloves yet. I told her there was no need to hurry. I got Appleby quite interested in your convalescence. And, goodness knows, there are not many sensible things Appleby is interested in.'

'I don't intend to go out yet. The gloves can wait. And I can be properly ill later on. I'll feel exhausted and go to bed early after the visitor has gone, if we have a visitor.'

'Very well,' sighed Vinetta. 'I suppose that will have to do. I've tidied the hall again. Tell the twins to make less noise or to go out and play in the back garden. Soobie will tell us if anybody is coming.'

At that moment Soobie's plump face appeared at the lounge door. He gave both of his parents a dour look and muttered, 'She's coming.'

'Who's coming?' asked Vinetta in the most natural way.

'Well it's not the meter reader so you needn't rush for your dark glasses.'

'Don't be funny,' said Vinetta sharply. 'I'll ask you again. Who's coming?'

'You know who's coming. Nobody else ever pays us a visit,' replied Soobie bluntly.

'You shouldn't say things like that, Soobie. Anybody could come. So, who have you seen coming up the drive?'

Just then the doorbell rang. Vinetta took a quick look at herself in the hall mirror and patted her neat black hair.

'I wonder who that can be,' she mused pointedly.

'It's Miss Quigley,' hissed the blue Mennym. 'You know fine well it is.'

Vinetta ignored him and went to open the door. Joshua, having silenced the twins, fled upstairs to make himself presentable to face a very prim maiden lady.

'Hortensia!' gushed Vinetta. 'This is a surprise! How lovely of you to have come, especially on such a cold day. Do come in and sit by the fire.'

Vinetta graciously led the way into the lounge where a leather three-piece suite was arranged round the gas fire. In front of the settee was a long low table, nicely carved round the rim and down the legs, and with a well-polished top.

Vinetta gave a warning look at Soobie who had gone back to his chair in the window and was reading a magazine. Then, having seen that her visitor was sitting comfortably, she went out to fetch the tea. The tray was always kept set in the pantry with china tea cups, milk jug, sugar basin, and a plate of aging biscuits.

Vinetta waited a reasonable time to allow for the boiling of a kettle and the brewing of the tea. Then, that pretend completed, she carried the tray carefully to the table before the fire.

'How nice,' simpered Miss Quigley. 'I always love that willow-pattern china. And those little pink biscuits are my favourites. You know what a sweet tooth I have!'

Vinetta passed the plate and Miss Quigley took one old biscuit and pretended to nibble at it genteelly. She took a satisfied sip from the invisible tea Vinetta had poured. Then she put the biscuit down again and brushed a non-existent crumb from her upper lip.

'I passed the Jarmans' on the way here,' said Miss Quigley confidentially. 'She was peeping out of her window again. I don't know how people can be so nosy. And I just got inside the gate when Mrs England passed with her Labrador. I was pleased I missed her. She is such a gossip.'

Miss Quigley's wide-brimmed hat did shadow her doll's face, but there was no way she could have spoken intimately to the neighbours without being detected. She knew that well enough, but it would have been so delightful to have stood swapping tales with people. The next best thing was a sour grapes pretend.

'I'm so pleased you came today,' said Vinetta. 'I have such a lot to tell you. You'll never believe all the things that have been happening here. The past week has been more eventful than many a year.'

Miss Quigley listened eagerly to the story of Joshua and the rat. She was truly horrified, but at the same time utterly fascinated. It was true. Things like that do not happen every day, or even every year.

'How will you manage?' she asked with concern when told that Joshua had lost his job.

'Oh, we do have some savings,' said Vinetta proudly, 'and the cheque they sent was quite substantial. I still earn money from the dressmaking.

Tulip has her own little business venture. And then, of course, Magnus is very well paid, though Joshua doesn't like to depend too much on his father. He has his pride.'

'He'll soon get another situation,' said Miss Quigley soothingly. 'They'll be wanting a Santa Claus at Peachum's soon. He did that a few years ago, didn't he?'

'Six years ago, to be precise, but they did ask him to go back the following year. They were very pleased with his work.'

Joshua came into the lounge dressed in his new trousers and a grey turtle-necked sweater.

'Good afternoon, Miss Quigley,' he said in as pleasant a voice as he could muster. He sat in the armchair to the left of the fire and poured himself a pretend cup of tea.

'Vinetta will have told you about my leg,' he added.

'Yes, indeed, Mr Mennym. It must have been a dreadful experience. I was so sorry to hear of it. I hope you are feeling better now.'

'Improving,' said Joshua, 'slowly improving, but I still need a lot of rest.'

At that moment, Wimpey, in the playroom, landed on Park Lane where Poopie had built a hotel. Her shriek startled the grown-ups, but she must have remembered the visitor. She darted into the lounge, said sorry, and quickly darted out again.

Vinetta passed without comment to her next piece of news.

'There is something else I have to tell you. It is more serious than Joshua's misfortune.'

Miss Quigley looked suitably startled. Surely there could be nothing more serious than having one's leg chewed to pieces by a rat and then losing one's job in the next breath.

Vinetta explained all about the letter from Albert Pond. Poor Miss Quigley stared wide-eyed. She lost her grip on the pretend. This Australian, whoever he was, owned the house. He owned the house! He even owned Miss Quigley's cupboard and she felt sure that he would not stick to the rules.

'How terrible!' she cried and fell in a heap on the floor.

'She's fainted,' said Soobie from his seat by the window. 'That's not a pretend.' He did not stir from his seat nor offer to help, but, having told his parents a simple fact that they might have missed, he went back to reading his magazine.

Tulip came from the breakfast room to see what all the fuss was about. She had her knitting needles in her hand and her reading glasses perched on the end of her nose. She regarded Miss Quigley as Vinetta's friend and usually stayed out of the way whenever she visited.

'What's the matter with her?' she demanded in her usual brusque voice. Without more ado, she put her needles down on the bureau and was ready to help.

'Come on. Help her up. You can't just leave her lying there.'

They helped Miss Quigley on to the settee, patted her hands and her painted cheeks and tried hard to revive her. Soobie picked up her broad-brimmed hat and fanned her face vigorously. Slowly she came round, and when she was more or less herself again, she looked totally embarrassed.

'I can't think what came over me,' she fluttered. 'It must be the heat of the fire. I'd best be going now anyway. I'm glad we don't have Australians to worry about in Trevethick Street. It's my own house, you know. Father left it to me. I'll call again next week, my dear, to see how things are.'

She left very formally by the front door after shaking hands with Joshua and kissing Vinetta lightly on the cheek. Tulip held back from any farewell greeting and looked for once very much the unapproachable Lady Mennym. It was clear that she disapproved of fainting and was offended by the silly woman's remarks about the house in Trevethick Street.

The door closed. Ten minutes later Miss Quigley slipped in at the back entrance and went unobserved to her own private cupboard.

8. Sir Magnus Calls a Meeting

SIR MAGNUS Mennym lay propped up on his pillows with his portable desk across his lap. The purple foot dangled nonchalantly from the counterpane. Its owner was still but not sleeping. He had just finished composing a crossword puzzle for *The Times* and was pausing to contemplate. (7 across: think with a pattern to study first maybe.)

Suddenly he took the stout cane that stood at the left-hand side of his pillow and knocked quite vigorously on the floor. When no one came, he knocked again but twice as hard.

'What on earth is the matter?' cried Vinetta dashing up the stairs and into the bedroom.

'Send for them all,' said her father-in-law impressively and ponderously.

Vinetta was so startled she forgot about the terrible knocking that threatened the ceilings below, and just echoed Sir Magnus's last word.

'All?'

'All,' he repeated. Then he reflected a little more. 'All except Googles and, of course, Miss Quigley, unless she happens to be paying us a visit today.'

'No,' said Vinetta, 'she was just here on Tuesday. She said she would be coming back some day next week.'

'Where's Tulip? I might as well not have a wife for all I see of her!'

'She's in the breakfast room doing the bills. She's always busy, you know, Magnus. And she is the only one in the house who can manage the accounts. Soobie could do it, but he won't.'

'Appleby could make little rings round all of you,' said her grandfather defensively. 'Let her loose on the accounts . . .'

'Let her loose on the accounts,' interrupted Vinetta realistically, 'and we'd have every teenage novelty on the market and nothing in the bank. I'll go and fetch Tulip.'

'And Appleby and Soobie – and even the terrible twins. Tell my son he'd better come too, though goodness knows what he'll have to contribute. We'll all have to talk it out and make some sort of decision.'

Vinetta did not ask any questions. She just hurried away and told all of the others to come to Granpa's room.

'What does he want this time?' grumbled Appleby. 'I got the papers for him this morning and I'm going to the Post Office for him this afternoon.'

'I don't know what he wants, but I'm guessing it will be something to do with the letter from Australia.'

'Oh that!' said Appleby, swinging her legs back and forward where she sat on the stool in front of her dressing-table mirror. She was trying hard to look as if she weren't interested, but she couldn't quite manage it. After forty years of increasingly awkward adolescence, she still had not achieved perfect boredom.

Poopie and Wimpey were in the playroom. Poopie was engaged in making his Action Man slide down a rope into the jungle. Wimpey, ignoring him completely, was reading, probably for the twentieth time, a very old copy of *Where the Rainbow Ends*. They were both pleased to be invited to a family conference. Usually they were considered to be too young for that sort of thing.

When Tulip was summoned, she took her time putting everything neatly in its proper place. The file on her desk had compartments for every sort of account. The work basket she had 'inherited' from Aunt Kate was full of different coloured wools, but not a single strand was out of place, not a single skein was tangled.

'I'll be there in a minute,' she said, resenting all of the minutes she was going to lose, and into her canvas bag she put the cardigan she was busy making. If they must have a family conference, then at least she could do something useful whilst they all sat talking. If Magnus expected her to be the attentive and dignified Lady Mennym, then he had another think coming.

Soobie was even more awkward.

'I'm not coming,' he said flatly. 'It will be another of his stupid pretends and I'm fed up with them. What is it this time? Is he making a will to send to his solicitor?'

'That's not fair,' protested Vinetta. 'It is not all pretend. We are real, aren't we?'

'I think,' said Soobie sarcastically, 'therefore it is self-evident that I am. And at least I know what I am, which is more than the rest of you do. I am a blue rag doll that, God knows how, can think and move. I do not eat or drink. I don't know what being hungry or thirsty means. I do not mix with human beings. And I know that Miss Quigley lives in the hall cupboard.'

Vinetta looked shocked.

'That is very, very cruel,' she said. 'I thought you were kinder than that. We may be what you said we were, but we don't just think and move. We have feelings as well and they can be hurt.'

Soobie looked ashamed of himself.

'I'm sorry,' he said. 'You're right, of course. There is no need for me to take it out on others because I feel sad. It is just that I find it hard to accept being a rag doll in a world that is obviously designed for human beings.'

'So we pretend to be human beings,' coaxed Vinetta. 'I know it's not perfect, but it helps. It has worked, more or less, for forty years. It has its benefits too. We never grow any older.'

She glanced at her own face in the mirror above the fireplace. A middle-aged face, but quite neat and pretty, framed by black wavy hair and lit up by flecked blue button eyes into which her personality had projected lively intelligence. A caring face, with little worry lines around the mouth and a short frown between the eyebrows. It had looked exactly the same when she had first observed it forty years before.

Soobie looked at her lovingly. He knew she was a good mother, fussy maybe, over-anxious perhaps, but good.

'I wish I could pretend,' he tried to explain, 'but I can't. I have to look at things as they are.'

Vinetta tried another tack.

'I don't think Granpa wants us for another pretend anyway. I think he wants a conference about the letter from Australia. That was real enough and it poses a real enough threat.'

'Very well,' said Soobie reluctantly. 'I'll come.'

He got stiffly out of the loom chair that stood at the right-hand side of the bay window, facing outwards to the garden and the street beyond. He usually sat there all day and every day. At night he did go to bed in his own room because rag dolls can sleep. He also sponged himself down in the mornings to keep the dust from gathering on his face and striped suit. Sometimes he would allow Vinetta to wash his clothes completely. At such times he would stay in bed till the clothes were washed, dried and aired. In his whole life he had only twice had new sets of clothing. Then he had insisted that they must be faithful copies of the originals. Not for Soobie the fashion fads of his sister Appleby. The blue face and the blue-striped suit were himself.

9. The Conference

SOOBIE and Vinetta arrived last at Granpa's room.

'Took you long enough,' the old man grumbled. 'You sit there, Vinetta.' He pointed to the only chair left empty in the room. 'And you, Soobie, can just sit yourself on the floor. Here's a cushion.'

So saying, Magnus flung the cushion at Soobie with such vigour that it knocked him over and Poopie and Wimpey, sitting side by side on the ottoman, laughed nervously.

'Serves you right,' said Granpa. 'You shouldn't have kept us waiting.'

Joshua was sitting on a stiff-backed chair near the door. He had made up his mind to say nothing. His anxious wife and domineering father were just too much for him. The loss of his comfortable, lonely job still hung over him like a cloud.

Appleby was leaning against the end of Granpa's bed, sensibly away from the dangling foot, though, as the favourite grandchild, it is doubtful whether she would ever have been treated to the force of it.

Tulip, Lady Mennym, was sitting in the big armchair studying her own, neatly written knitting pattern before resuming work on the cardigan in her lap. It was not for any member of the family. It was part of her own little business venture. Posted off to Harrods, as others had been before, it would be sold as an exclusive creation and make more money to pay the never-ending bills. Minor royalty and fashion models had worn the 'tulipmennym' label and recommended it to those friends of theirs who could afford it.

Granpa looked at her and gritted his moustache. She obviously was not paying attention but at least she had come.

'Now,' said Granpa ominously, 'first things first. What do you think about Albert Pond's letter?'

Nobody spoke.

'Joshua?' queried the old man looking determinedly in his son's direction.

'Not much,' said Joshua with economy.

'What sort of an answer's that?' asked Magnus with growing irritation.

Silence.

Poopie stared hard at Granpa. His blue button eyes were very round and innocent. His straight yellow fringe touched the top of his eyebrows. His small mouth struggled as he made the effort to put a thought into words.

'Why does he think being a Sir is so important, Granpa?' he said at last in a puzzled little voice. 'Why are you a Sir?' In all of forty years he had not given this a thought.

Sir Magnus, for once, looked uncomfortable. Truth to tell, he hadn't the faintest idea why he was Sir. Being born aged seventy, there were many things he did not know about himself when young. The memory built into him had not included any information about his knighthood. Memory is so capriciously selective. What made it even more difficult was that Kate, or whoever was responsible, had not made him a natural liar. So to make up a story about it and tell it with conviction was more than he could manage at short notice.

Appleby came to the rescue.

'He's called Sir Magnus,' she said airily, 'because the Queen gave him a knighthood for his services to journalism and the reports he sent home from trouble spots in the world when he was a young man. Did you not know he was in Egypt at the time of the Suez Crisis?'

Sir Magnus gave his granddaughter a look of deep admiration. It had the makings of a classic pretend. But he felt it was risky to let her go any further.

'Young man's stuff,' he said deprecatingly. 'No good living in the past.'

'But what's a knighthood?' persisted Poopie, still looking eagerly from beneath his yellow fringe like a little dog hot on the scent of a bone.

'The question is irrelevant,' snapped Granpa. Had the unfortunate Poopie been within range of the purple foot he would undoubtedly have been thumped against the wall.

'What is relevant,' he continued quickly, 'is this young man's proposal to pay us a visit. How do we stop him?'

'Ignore the letter,' said Soobie. 'If we don't answer he'll assume that we haven't received it, or that, if we have, we don't want to know.'

'We do not know what he would assume,' insisted Sir Magnus, 'and even if he made either of the assumptions you suppose, that would not stop him from dropping in unexpectedly one of these days.'

'He doesn't sound like the sort of young man who would come without warning,' said Vinetta anxiously. 'He sounds too sensitive and considerate.'

Sir Magnus would not be deflected.

'We must assume, Vinetta, that unless we dissuade him, there is every possibility that he will come. So how do we dissuade him?'

Appleby, without any by-your-leave, snatched the letter from under Granpa's hand. She had read it before. They all had. Now she read it again more slowly and more carefully.

'We need,' she mused, 'an unanswerable excuse for being absent from home for the whole of November.'

'We've never been absent from home in our lives. We're certainly not going to start now,' growled Soobie.

'We don't really need to go,' explained Appleby slyly. 'The absence will only be a pretend. Say we've booked a holiday in Cornwall. And, of course, we will omit to tell him precisely where.'

'A holiday in Cornwall in November!' scoffed Soobie. 'Your pretends aren't up to their usual high standards, Apples. I could do better than that and I don't even like pretends.'

'All right, young fellow,' snarled Granpa, 'if you're so clever, do better.'

Appleby gave Soobie a look of jealous fury. Just let him dare do better, the look said. Then, just as the atmosphere was becoming unbearably tense, and the purple foot was itching to kick someone or something, Appleby was visited by inspiration.

'I know,' she said. 'It's easy. We are going to fly to Canada on a month's visit to our cousins, Satty and Lodie. They have just had a new baby and we are all going over for the christening.'

'And who, may I ask, are Satty and Lodie?' demanded Soobie in a heavily sarcastic voice.

'Don't you ever listen to anything I say? I've just told you. They are our cousins. We haven't seen them for three years. Satty married Lodie in London three years ago. It was a real society wedding. We were all there. The twins were much smaller then and Lodie had them as flower-girl and page-boy. They wanted me to be bridesmaid but I couldn't because, even at twelve, I was taller than Lodie and I thought it would look silly. Googles wasn't even born then.'

'Hold on! Hold on!' cried Granpa. 'I don't think we need a whole family history. Still, the story does sound quite probable. You can write the letter, Appleby. I'll check it for errors and sign it. You can look on it as a piece of English homework. Geography too, for that matter. Whereabouts do they live in Canada?'

The purple foot had relaxed and was swinging carelessly and nearly touching the floor. Granpa, for once, was sitting bolt upright unsupported by his pillows and cushions. His attitude expressed his enthusiasm.

Without the least hesitation, Appleby said, 'Manitoba.' It was such a beautiful sounding name.

'Right,' said Granpa, with a twinkle in his black button eyes, 'see what you can find out about Manitoba before next Friday.'

Friday was Appleby's day for lessons with Granpa. She didn't know whether to be vexed or pleased.

'And you, Soobie,' Granpa began, but he got no further than that. Soobie jumped up off his velvet cushion and resisted the temptation to hurl it at somebody.

'I'm going,' said the blue Mennym forcefully, his silver eyes glinting. 'I've had enough of this.

You can make fools of yourselves if you like, but you're not going to make a fool of me.'

Joshua, without moving from his chair, leant over and opened the door to let Soobie escape. As he strutted out, his father gave him a look of deep accord. Joshua's amber lozenge eyes hid more than they revealed. He usually kept his grizzled head down and his chin tucked into his neck, a bit like a monk bent over his breviary. All he ever wanted was to be left in peace. Was that too much to ask?

Tulip put down her knitting and looked round the room after Soobie had left.

'I'm sure I don't know what this family's coming to,' she scolded. 'We can never have a conference without somebody walking out in a huff.'

'Somebody is nearly always Soobie,' said Appleby spitefully, 'and I wish he'd stop calling me Apples. He knows I hate it.'

Joshua made up his mind to speak, though it went against the grain.

'Let's call it a day,' he said firmly. 'Appleby can write the letter. I think it should come from me rather than Father. The young man obviously hasn't worked out our ages and we don't want complications in years to come. In their terms, Father could easily be a hundred and ten.'

10. A Letter to Australia

Dear Albert,

I hope you don't mind if I call you by your first name. You sound so friendly, I'm beginning to think of you as part of the family. We all are.

My father received your kind letter and showed it to us. We would, of course, be delighted to meet you. I am writing this on behalf of us all, from the oldest to the youngest.

Unfortunately, at the time you are going to be in England, the house will be closed up completely. The whole family is going on a long overdue visit to our cousins in Manitoba. They have just had their first child after three years of marriage. We are flying out there next Tuesday to be present at the christening. It has all been arranged for weeks. We will not be returning to Brocklehurst Grove till Christmas, by which time you will doubtless be back home after your trip.

Coincidence is strange, isn't it? We haven't even been away on holiday for the past three years. Yet here we are, booked to go, just at a time when we would have much preferred to be here to meet you.

There is much to be said for family life, Albert. You say you have no intention of marrying yet. Let me, in a fatherly way, advise you. I married Vinetta seventeen years ago and it is the one step I have never regretted. Find yourself a nice girl and settle down. Thirty is just the right age for a man to marry. I'm sure there must be some really pleasant girls out there who would, as they say, fall for your charms as we already have. You sound a thoroughly agreeable lad.

Yours very sincerely,
Joshua Mennym

The reluctant Joshua was made to copy Appleby's effort out in his painstakingly slow hand. He was no writer. When it came to signing his name at the end, he was relieved, of course, but he felt very uncomfortable.

'It doesn't sound like me,' he grumbled.

'It doesn't need to,' said Vinetta patiently. 'He will never know what you sound like – which is just as well considering how little you have to say for yourself. Appleby's made a good job of that letter. I like the bit about marriage.'

'You would,' growled Joshua.

'Don't you see?' explained Vinetta. 'If he marries he'll be more settled. He'll not want to travel the world in search of friendly Mennyms.'

'Or unfriendly ones,' said Soobie, on his father's side as usual. 'Let's get the thing posted and be done with it.'

It was put into an airmail envelope, stamped and sealed down.

'I hope we've put enough stamps on,' worried Vinetta.

'Of course we have,' said Appleby with total assurance. She knew about these things.

'I'll post it on my way to the Market,' said her mother, anxious as usual to have everything done and dusted.

'No!' said Appleby hastily. 'I'll post it. Posting letters is my job. I'm going to the Post Office this afternoon in any case.'

She seized the finished letter and thrust it into her jeans pocket.

'Mind what you're doing with it,' fussed Vinetta, 'and don't forget to post it.'

'I never forget anything,' said Appleby airily. 'Just ask Granpa.'

Wimpey had been watching them quietly and dreamily.

'If we write to him he might write to us again. He might send us something for Christmas. I would like a koala bear. Granpa says koala bears live in Australia.'

'Silly,' mocked Poopie, 'you can't send animals through the post. It would die.'

Wimpey blushed but looked cross at the same time. She flung her fair curls back and glared at her brother.

'I didn't mean a live one,' and, before Poopie could make any jokes about dead ones, she added, 'I meant a toy one like my teddy bear.'

11. Joshua's Christmas Job

TULIP was doing the accounts. She always sat at a little old desk in the corner of the breakfast room to do this very important job on the third Thursday of every month.

Joshua had been out of work for nearly four weeks. Magnus was waiting for payment for three of his articles on The Early Battles of the English Civil War, a subject in which he specialised. Vinetta had sold four children's dresses to a small local dress shop, but it was, as usual, on a sale-or-return basis. So until the dresses were actually sold she would receive no money. Harrods would have only just received the three cardigans Tulip had sent them. They were prompt payers, but nobody pays by return post. There was still money in the bank, but Tulip was very careful. She liked each month to meet its own expenses. She also refused to regard Joshua's redundancy money as income. It was a lump sum, wasn't it? Well, lump sums should be put away for special outlay, not for the bits and pieces of everyday living. That was how they managed, over the years, to buy television sets, a typewriter for Magnus, a more modern sewing machine for Vinetta, new overcoats for Joshua, good toys for the children at Christmas and birthdays, and many other expensive items.

Tulip added up the figures and frowned. So much had gone on gas, electricity, wool, thread, cloth, cleaning materials. And this month there was the telephone bill. Calls were strictly business, but if appearing in person is fraught with difficulties, the telephone is not a luxury but a dire necessity. A rag doll on the telephone sounds just like anybody else.

Tulip looked thoughtful. She pressed the brass bell on her desk. It was meant to summon Joshua, but it did not often produce the desired effect.

'Dad!' shouted Soobie from his usual seat in the lounge, 'can't you hear the bell? Gran wants you. It's the third Thursday.'

Joshua was sitting on the stairs feeling bored and sorry for himself. He liked going out to work. He was used to going out to work. It made the time at home so much more pleasant.

'I'm coming,' he called. 'I'm coming. No need to go on about it.'

He went into the breakfast room where his mother was still irritatingly tinkling away at the little bell as if it were the triangle in the orchestra.

'Stop that, Mother,' snapped Joshua. 'I'm here now. What is it you want?'

Without a word she thrust the accounts at him. He glanced at them in a puzzled fashion.

'Looks all right to me,' he said with his usual brevity and ran his fingers through his dull brown hair. It was well-made hair. It even had grey streaks at the temples and above the forehead.

Tulip gave her son a withering look. Her crystal eyes could look very glassy on occasions.

'The sums are all correct,' she said drily. 'Arithmetic is one of the things I do well. But even to your unpractised eyes it should be clear that we have done badly this month. More out, less in, is not satisfactory.'

Joshua looked at her, still not enlightened.

'I think you have recuperated for long enough, Josh,' said Tulip at last. 'Here.'

She passed him the previous night's copy of the local paper, opened at the Situations Vacant and with the appropriate vacancy circled in red. She felt that she had to be cruel to be kind.

Joshua read it.

'They want a Santa Claus at Peachum's,' he said flatly.

'They'll take you like a shot. Get Vinetta to stitch the white whiskers on again. That's why they liked you the last time. Real whiskers are much better than those that just hook on round the ears.'

Joshua looked very reluctant.

'I don't like the job,' he said, 'and that's the truth. I didn't like it last time. I was glad I was working when they sent for me the following year. I don't like the whiskers and the bushy eyebrows.'

'But you do like the money,' explained his mother, 'and we need more coming in than we have at present. You used to be a hard worker. Now you just seem content to sit on the stairs with your chin in your hands. It's not good for you – and it's not good for the rest of us either.'

That stung. Joshua felt angry at the unfairness of her words, but he did not argue.

'I'll go,' he said coldly. 'Get Appleby to write the usual letter. I see you've made your mind up.'

'She'll remind them that you did the job before and how pleased they were. You won't even have to have an interview. They'll just make you an offer in the post.'

'I suppose so,' said Joshua with no enthusiasm at all.

Tulip sighed.

'If I'd been a man,' she said, 'I'd have loved being Santa Claus. Seeing all those children happy with their Christmas wishes, clutching their little toys. And you couldn't find a job where you would be better hidden. The beard, the hood, the bushy brows and the red cheeks are a perfect disguise.'

Joshua got to the door before he muttered, 'Greedy little brats with loud voices and sticky fingers.'

'I may have cloth ears,' said his mother tartly, 'but I did hear that. Not all humans are nasty and grasping. The very young are still full of wonder and well you know it!'

He did know it. As he sat beneath the tree in Peachum's, nice mums with nice children came to see him as if they all believed he was real. Cross mums with fractious children came too, but they were not the majority by any means.

One wet day, three figures wearing thick raincoats with hoods pulled well down over their heads, even inside the shop, came gleefully to the grotto.

'Now,' said Santa to the small boy who sidled up to him, 'what can I bring you this year?'

Poopie giggled discreetly into his collar.

'I want a train set,' he mumbled.

'Speak up, son,' said Joshua, putting one arm round the lad's shoulder.

'I want a train set, Dad,' laughed Poopie, looking boldly up at Joshua so that he could see the face inside the hood.

'Get out of here,' hissed Santa with unSantalike venom. 'Do you want us all to be found out?'

He looked at the little girl in red who stood behind Poopie and realised that it was Wimpey. The tall, thin teenager with her hand on Wimpey's shoulder could only be Appleby.

'All it needs now is Soobie,' groaned Joshua.

'That'll be the day!' mocked Appleby. 'He's never left the house since . . .'

Whatever Appleby was going to say was interrupted. A real child standing behind her was growing impatient and began to push. With great presence of mind, Joshua thrust tissue paper parcels into the twins' hands, blue for Poopie, pink for Wimpey, and ushered them on.

'Well, little lad,' said Santa to the dour-faced five-year-old who had done the pushing, 'what would you like me to bring you this year?'

'A monster,' said the child, 'a proper one with goggle eyes and a battery.'

His mother smiled nervously at Santa's hood.

'I'll see what we can do,' said Santa diplomatically. 'Just wait till Christmas morning, but in the meantime, ho-ho, what have we here for you in my barrel of fun?'

The child dipped right down into the barrel and rummaged in the bottom as if all the best presents might be hidden.

'Blue for a boy, pink for a girl,' said Santa when the lad emerged with a pink parcel, which he hastily threw back and set about diving again and rummaging. Not one of the nicer children!

That evening Joshua fumed at Appleby.

'Don't you ever, ever do that again. Do you want me to lose my job?'

'There was no harm done,' said Appleby. 'We're entitled to a bit of fun. We are not all like you and Soobie.'

'More's the pity,' said Joshua.

He sat down to his make-believe dinner and drank without relish his pretend mug of tea. They were entitled to a bit of fun. Rag dolls have as much right to Christmas as anybody. Joshua's anger left him and he felt saddened by his thoughts.

Soobie, the blue Mennym, sat still in his chair by the window and, thinking on what had been said, cried inside himself because they were not human and no amount of pretending would ever make them so.

'We can always pretend,' he said at last, bitterly and grudgingly, but with determination. 'We will be having the tree and presents as usual. At least the presents will be real.'

'There's a cardboard turkey at the store,' said Joshua. 'Nobody'll miss it. I'll sneak it home on Christmas Eve.'

'Are you sure that's all right?' asked Vinetta anxiously. 'Sounds a bit dishonest to me.'

'Of course it's all right,' said her husband. 'It's the sort of thing they throw away when the holiday is over.'

Vinetta looked reassured and began to feel enthusiastic about the latest pretend.

'We'll set the table like they do in books. I could buy some real fruit. It won't matter that we can't actually eat it. I might even get a bottle of wine and we can get out Aunt Kate's wine glasses. Then there's the damask tablecloth we've only used once – the last time we celebrated Appleby's fifteenth birthday.'

Vinetta was feeling happier herself and the others became more cheerful too.

'I'll write a note to Miss Quigley and invite her for Christmas dinner.'

'Oh no!' protested Joshua. 'Let's pretend she's celebrating Christmas in her own home this year.'

'No,' said Vinetta firmly. 'It is Christmas after all. A time of good will. Aunt Kate would be so sad if she knew that poor Miss Quigley was supposed to spend Christmas alone in Trevethick Street.'

Soobie was beginning to feel sorry he had set them off on this pretend. He resisted the temptation to mention the hall cupboard.

'At least,' he said bleakly, if somewhat irrelevantly, 'when you feel sad, you are feeling something. That is real enough.'

When Christmas Day finally came, they all enjoyed it. The real presents were purchased at a generous staff discount from Peachum's. Everybody got something nice and new, shawls, slippers, books, a train set and a real doll for a doll that wasn't real.

'It can talk,' said Wimpey when she pulled out the string at the back.

'I'm-Polly,' grated the doll in a flat voice with a distinct American accent. 'What-are-you-called? Would-you-like-a-Chocolate-Milk?'

This appealed to Appleby, who took up the accent immediately and kept on asking them if they would like a Chocolate Milk till they all screamed at her to stop.

'Settle down and be more quiet, all of you,' said Vinetta when the squabbling had gone on too long. 'You're upsetting Googles. And I don't know what Miss Quigley must be thinking of you.'

Miss Quigley was sitting on a high-backed chair near the lounge door. She had her presents clutched on her knee.

'They're just a bit over-excited,' she said. 'It has been a lovely Christmas. I've never had a nicer lunch.'

She stood up and pushed the presents into her large shopping bag.

'I'm afraid I will have to be going now,' she said. 'It's getting dusk. My poor little cat will be thinking I'm lost. Thank you for everything.'

Vinetta took her to the front door. They all called their goodbyes, apart from Soobie, who was reading his Christmas book, and Tulip who was busy in the kitchen, up to her elbows in rubber gloves and soap suds. The dishes that were taking up so much of her attention were already clean, of course, but washing them was a nice, solitary occupation, and even clean dishes can be made to shine a bit more brightly.

Ten minutes later the back door opened quietly and Miss Quigley tiptoed past Tulip and slipped into the hall cupboard. This time nobody, not even Appleby, gave any sign that they had seen her.

12. Albert's Second Letter

'WHAT on earth are you doing?'
Vinetta stood at the top of the stairs and looked down at Appleby who had trudged snow into the hall and was busily, guiltily, trying to cover the traces. It was seven-thirty on Saturday morning in the middle of January.

'Nothing,' said Appleby, giving herself time to think.

Vinetta came down the stairs, still in her dressing-gown, and eyed her daughter suspiciously.

'And what might nothing be?' she demanded.

'I went out the back door to look at the snow and when I came back in I saw the postman had been and I went to pick up the letters and I forgot I had snow on my boots and I . . .'

'And why are you up this early?' interrupted her mother. 'It's not even daylight yet. I doubt if you have ever seen the world before at this time of the morning.'

Appleby looked only slightly embarrassed, then plunged on with her explanations.

'It was so cold in my room I couldn't sleep and I got up and got dressed. That's all. I don't need anybody's permission to do that, do I?' she asked vigorously, finding her usual form. 'Then I thought, since I was up and dressed, I might as well go and see how much snow had fallen. I thought about making a snowman to surprise Poopie and Wimpey but I got a bit nervous out there in the dark.'

It was a plausible explanation. Vinetta shrugged and put her hand out for the letters Appleby was holding.

'One from Harrods. Gran will be pleased,' commented Vinetta, looking down at the top of five or six envelopes. The next was a bill, and the next. Then there was one for Sir Magnus, obviously from a publisher. Finally, with a start, Vinetta came to the last envelope. It was an airmail letter. The stamp was Australian. It was addressed, in a neat handwriting that by now looked very familiar, to Mr Joshua Mennym and Family.

'As if we haven't enough worries,' said Vinetta.

'I think I'll go back to bed,' yawned Appleby, making for the stairs.

'That's right,' said Vinetta tartly. 'I don't suppose we'll see you again till teatime now. I bet this hour's been a shock to your system!'

'No need to be sarcastic!' snapped Appleby. 'I can't do right for doing wrong in this house!' So saying, she flounced back upstairs to her own room and banged the door shut behind her.

Vinetta sighed. She went into the dark lounge, switched on the light, turned on the gas fire and sat in her favourite armchair. She put all of the letters, except the Australian one, in the brass letter-rack on the bureau. The letter from Albert Pond she opened apprehensively. She extracted the two flimsy blue sheets and let the envelope flutter to the floor.

Dear Joshua and all of you,

I can't say how pleased I was to get such a friendly letter from my English family, for that's what I think of you as now. I delayed replying because I knew you would be in Canada and I reckoned there wasn't much point in writing to your doormat!

Can't say how sorry I was that you had to go away just at the time when I had all but arranged to visit.

As it happens, it turned out for the best after all. Mate of mine from Queensland decided on a Christmas wedding and asked me to be best man. We go way back – kids at school together. So I didn't like to refuse. In fact, to be honest with you, I was delighted. Never thought Dewey would ever want to settle down, bit like me really, a born loner, but he'd met this nice girl who works in the City Library and they hit it off right away. She's called Edna, but she can't help that. She don't look like an Edna. She's tall and elegant with long blonde hair and a very sweet face. Dewey's a real lucky fellow.

I'll bear in mind what you said about finding a wife, but I'm afraid I'm like a lot of Aussies. I'll just hang around till someone decides to marry me. Course, I would have to hit it off with her, like Dewey with Edna. But I'm not going looking. It's not in my nature.

The wedding turned out to be really something. It took place on Boxing Day. The weather was sweltering. Edna's folks have this real big house with a lovely stretch of lawn. They had two huge marquees on the lawns, one for the food and one for the fun! There was dancing to an eight-piece band and there must have been getting on for five hundred guests. Probably doesn't seem much to you, but to me that is some big party!

Now the jamboree's over. They've gone on honeymoon to Japan of all places. And I'm back home here sorting out a few things and making a few plans. The station has a good manager in Toby Masters (fellow in his fifties, been with Uncle Ches for years and more than happy to stay on, especially as he knows I know I can trust him and will give him no trouble). So I'm sparing myself these two months away that I planned earlier. I'm having a lazy beach holiday in March and I'm really looking forward to spending April in England.

They tell me I'd do better to wait till June or July weatherwise, but weather's never bothered me much. If you're a slave to the calendar, you don't get so much fun out of life.

I hope that you and all your family are keeping well, especially the old folks. My own pa died ten years back and I lost my ma when I was fifteen. I've never been really lonely though. I'm not the type. But a jolly family, three generations in one big house, is something to admire.

Can't say how much I look forward to seeing you all. I'll send you more details of when I'll be coming after I've made all the arrangements. In the meantime, perhaps you'll find time to send me a line or two. Hoping you enjoyed your Christmas and are having a happy New Year,

Kindest regards,
Albert

Vinetta stooped down and picked the envelope off the floor. Carefully she folded the pages and put them back. Her lips were tense with worry. The clock on the mantelpiece said ten past eight.

'Ten past eight,' she sighed, 'and I'm not even dressed yet. What a start to the day!'

13. More Problems

'WHAT are we to do?'

Vinetta pulled the cords to open Granpa's curtains. It was ten o'clock and the winter sun streamed in. Outside was a brilliant white world. Inside it was a bit shivery, but beginning to warm up with the heat from Granpa's two-bar electric fire that Vinetta had thoughtfully switched on even before she let the light into the room. The counterpane, she noticed, was carefully draped over the foot that still protruded over the side of the bed.

Vinetta handed Granpa the letter as he grunted into consciousness and pulled himself up higher on his pillows. He read it quickly without a word. Then, still without speaking, he slid it back into the envelope.

'Has Joshua read it?' he then demanded.

'No, of course not. He's still sleeping. I never wake him up before ten-thirty on a Saturday.'

'It's addressed to him,' said Granpa huffily. 'He should have had it first by rights.'

'It's addressed to all of us,' explained Vinetta. 'We are included in the "and Family", aren't we?'

'Only Joshua is mentioned by name,' insisted Sir Magnus a little jealously.

'That's because Joshua's name was on the letter we wrote. Remember, we thought it safest to keep you in the background.'

Sir Magnus gave her a grumpy look but contented himself with saying, 'I suppose so.'

'Well,' said Vinetta, going back to her original question, 'what are we going to do?'

'Not much we can do,' said Granpa in a defeated voice. 'Get the others up here and see what we come up with if we pool our ideas.'

At that moment Tulip came in. She had been downstairs in the breakfast room since eight-thirty and had already read Albert's letter.

'What do you make of it?' she asked, nodding at the envelope Sir Magnus was still holding. 'Not much use telling him another string of lies. We're cornered this time, and no mistake.'

'Get the others,' barked Sir Magnus, glowering at his little wife. They were cornered, true enough, but rubbing it in didn't help.

Only Appleby failed to appear.

Soobie came from his chair in the lounge. Poopie and Wimpey came in from the back garden, somewhat reluctantly, with soggy hands and still wearing their damp wellingtons.

'Out of here!' insisted Tulip. 'Go to your own rooms and change into slippers at once. You are dripping all over the carpet.'

When they returned, Appleby still had not appeared.

'Where's the brains of the family?' asked Granpa.

'Appleby?' queried Vinetta.

'Yes, who else? I'd hardly mean Googles or even Miss Quigley.'

'Appleby's fast asleep, Magnus,' said Vinetta. 'I tried to rouse her, but you know what she is like. She was prowling around very early this morning and now she looks set to sleep for a week.'

Had it been anybody else Granpa would have insisted on the offender being dragged sleeping into his presence. But not Appleby.

'Leave her,' said the old man charitably. 'When we've run out of ideas she'll come up with something fresh. She's as bright as a button.'

'I have ideas,' said Poopie. His eyes, bright blue button eyes, glared from under his yellow fringe. 'I have lots of ideas.'

'Well, let's hear them then,' said Granpa drily.

'We could close the curtains and lock the doors and windows and hide up here till he goes away.'

'Brilliant!' drawled Magnus and didn't even bother to explain how futile that would be.

'What about you, Soobie? Can you produce some stroke of genius?' Granpa's tone was just sarcastic enough to nettle the blue Mennym.

'You're supposed to be the one with all the pearls of wisdom,' Soobie said. 'Haven't you got one to fit this situation?'

Granpa looked furious. 'We'll have less of that, young man, or I'll have you put out in the snow.'

'Now, now,' said Vinetta soothingly, 'let's not get upset. Tell Granpa you are sorry, Soobie.'

Soobie's face turned bluer than ever as he suppressed his temper.

'I'm sorry,' he said in a voice that didn't sound sorry a bit.

Granpa chose to ignore the tone and said loftily, 'Your apology is graciously accepted. Now produce an idea.'

Soobie looked thoughtful.

'Not one of us has thought of anything sensible yet. The only thing I can say with certainty is that we will eventually. Necessity is the mother of invention. That is one of your pearls of wisdom, Granpa.' He kept a very straight face.

'Humph!' said Granpa. 'At least you are thinking. The rest of them are either numb or dumb.'

'Well,' said Soobie, 'for a start, I'll have to hide in the attic till he's gone. The rest of you might manage some sort of disguise, but a blue Mennym is impossible to pass off as human, even with glasses and a beard.'

At that moment, Appleby put in an appearance. Granpa's door opened wide to the wall and she flounced in.

'What am I missing?' she demanded in an accusing voice. She stood there looking all stiff knees and stiff elbows in a pose that was deliberately impudent. 'What are you all doing behind my back?'

Vinetta gave her a withering look. Joshua, more tolerant, was about to explain. Before he could speak, however, Sir Magnus raised himself up from his pillows and beckoned to his favourite in a friendly fashion.

'I hear you got up a bit too early this morning,' he said in tones far more pleasant than he would have used to any other latecomer. 'Feeling rested now?'

'Yes, Granpa,' replied Appleby sweetly. 'Now, what exactly is the problem?'

Granpa explained very briefly. He knew it was not necessary to hammer points home with Appleby. For all her little faults, she was a sharp lass, worth two of any of the others.

Appleby brightened.

'There's all sorts we can do. Soobie's right about hiding in the attic. We can put Googles there too, and Miss Quigley. I'm sure Miss Quigley could look after Googles and keep her quiet. That leaves Granpa, Granny Tulip, Dad and Mum, and Poopie and Wimpey. And me, of course!'

'I can be a spaceman with a helmet on,' said Poopie.

'Idiot!' said Appleby. 'That's no better than being a rag doll. Can you imagine what Albert would think if you stood there with a helmet on and never showed your face?'

Sir Magnus glowered at Poopie but said nothing.

'I could pretend to be a doll,' said Wimpey. 'I'm not as big as the rest of you. I can stay in the basket chair in Appleby's bedroom and if Albert Pond decides to look around the house, I know I could stay ever so still when he came to Appleby's room.'

'That's a good idea,' said Appleby, 'and Poopie will just have to go in the attic with the others. I'm not sure whether Albert Pond knows you two exist, but we'll tell him that the twins are at boarding school, just in case.'

'So far, so good,' said Granpa, chewing his moustache, 'but what about the ones who have to meet the fellow? How are we going to pass ourselves off?'

'You will stay in bed, Granpa,' said Appleby, as if he ever did anything else. 'We'll buy some thicker net curtains and we can keep the velvet ones nearly shut. You can have a pair of spectacles with lenses like bottle bottoms. That will hide your eyes. You can keep your hands under the counterpane. If you nod your head at him graciously he won't expect to shake hands.'

'What if it's dark when he comes? Electric light is very revealing.'

'Low watt bulbs. Dark lampshades. We might even get away with just having the bedside lamp lit. We can tell him that your eyes are troubling you.'

'What about the rest of us?' asked Vinetta. 'We can't all lie in bed and wear thick glasses.'

'You are speaking to someone who has been to the cinema hundreds of times, and even to the occasional disco. I can pass myself off as human with very little effort. I'll wear my dark glasses with the butterfly frames, all my mod clothes and the big hairy wig. I can even keep my multi-coloured gloves on. Teenagers these days can get away with anything. It is our world.' Appleby looked triumphant.

'And what about me and Dad?' insisted Vinetta. 'We are not teenagers.'

'No,' giggled Appleby. 'I must say I cannot see the two of you looking the part in my gear.'

'So we are stuck.'

'No, not really,' continued Appleby. 'We can have thick curtains and low watt bulbs all over the house. As for you, Mum, the least human thing about you is your eyes. I think you should wear a pair of blue-tinted spectacles. And maybe that high-necked dress with the frilled collar to shade your jawline. Your hands and your hair are beautiful.'

Vinetta's hands really were very good. They were one of Kate's major successes being complete with separate, well-formed fingers. Vinetta had long ago fixed false fingernails to their tips. It made shopping so much easier. But they still felt like cloth. Nothing could give them the feel of flesh.

'What if he shakes hands with me? He's sure to want to shake hands. It's something all humans do.'

'I've thought of a way round that. He'll only think of shaking hands when he first arrives and maybe when he leaves. You will answer the door to him with a tea towel in your hands and a few soap bubbles on your fingers. He'll be so apologetic about coming at an inconvenient time that the handshakes will be forgotten.'

'That leaves me,' said Joshua.

'Depends upon what time he arrives.' Appleby looked a bit stumped but wasn't going to give up too easily. Soobie might come up with some good idea and she didn't want that.

'If he comes during the day you can be out at work. You can pretend to work late and we'll try to get rid of him before you arrive.'

'And where will I *really* be, considering that I am unemployed? Not in the attic, I hope. A whole day of Miss Quigley is too much to ask.'

'No, Dad, not in the attic. You might have to come in and sneaking down from the attic might be awkward. You'll just have to stay quietly in the garden shed.'

'And if the fellow wants to look in the shed?'

'We'll say we've lost the key and we'll insist on finding it and he'll say not to bother. And we'll still insist. Then he'll look embarrassed and say he can't put us to all that trouble.'

Sir Magnus looked delighted.

'See how she pictures things! She's the one with the ideas! She's the one you'd be glad of if you were shipwrecked on a desert island.'

Appleby tried to look modest. Vinetta made a private resolve to tell Sir Magnus at some other time that he shouldn't say things to add to Appleby's conceit. The girl had a high enough opinion of herself to start with.

'But if the lad has to see me, how will we manage then?' Joshua looked worried. Even if he had been flesh and blood, meeting this stranger would have been an ordeal. Joshua was a very shy man.

'Mum will have to stitch you a black curly beard the way she made your white Santa Claus one. And even if it makes it look as if we are all weak-eyed, you'll have to wear thick spectacles. I'll buy a big horn-rimmed pair from the optician's on the High Street. His shop is small and badly lit. I think it must be like that to make his customers feel that their eyes really do need testing.'

'That's a point, though,' quibbled Joshua. 'He's sure to want to do an eye test before he sells you any glasses, especially thick ones.'

'No, he'll not,' said Appleby, producing yet another card from her sleeve. 'I've had them before. He thinks I am in an amateur dramatic group. So he sells me odd pairs cheap.'

'And how does he come to have odd pairs?' insisted Joshua, looking at her suspiciously.

'I didn't ask him. I suppose he might have samples or maybe some people order spectacles and don't come back to claim them.'

'Silly man,' said Granny Tulip, looking at them all sharply over the tops of her own little gold-rimmed glasses. 'He should charge a deposit. That would make people think twice about leaving stuff on his hands. You tell him that. Anyway, how about me, pet? You've missed me out – and a right fool I'd look in specs too big for my face.'

Appleby looked at her sharp-eyed little grandmother. Behind the clear lenses, the crystal beads that were her eyes were brilliant and almost magical.

'No problem,' said Appleby. 'You'll be busy all the time. You'll be in the corner of the breakfast room, sitting at your desk with bills in one hand and a pen in the other. You won't need to stand up. You won't need to shake hands. If he stays any length of time, you can slip in the lounge and join in the conversation.'

'And what about my eyes?' The crystals glinted above the small reading glasses, and her mouth had a faint but definitely mischievous smile.

Suddenly Appleby realised what she had never known before. It was staggering.

'You can take care of yourself, Gran. If he looks into your eyes, he won't know what's hit him. He'll be hypnotised. It won't matter after that what he sees.'

'Clever girl!' exclaimed Magnus. 'There, Tulip. It didn't take her long to find you out!'

'Only forty years,' said Tulip drily. 'We have made a bit of headway today, though. Now I have work to do, and if you don't mind, or even if you do, I'm away to get on with it.'

Before they all went about their business, Joshua, dour and dogmatic as usual, managed to get agreement on one point. They would ignore Albert's request for 'a few lines'. The fellow obviously didn't need any encouragement.

14. Joshua's Bliss

AT THE beginning of March, another meaningful, marvellous letter came for Joshua. Sydenham's wanted him back.

'They want me back if I am available,' he said happily.

'And are you available after the shabby way they treated you?' asked Vinetta pointedly. 'They did make you redundant, after all. Now they're having to eat their words. Serve them right if you turn them down.'

Joshua looked uncomfortable. It would serve them right. They'd had three successful break-ins since he had left and goodness knows how many unsuccessful attempts. The electronic security system was expensive and well known, so well known that the criminal fraternity had learned how to cope with it. An empty warehouse is an empty warehouse. A machine is no substitute for a man.

'But a rag doll is!' Joshua had chuckled as he read the letter.

Now, with Vinetta priming him to be spiteful, he wasn't sure what to do.

'I did mention it to Father,' he said defensively.

'And what did he say?' asked Vinetta.

'Pretty much the same as you at first, but then he was afflicted by a pearl of wisdom and told me I mustn't cut my nose off to spite my face.'

'In other words?' insisted Vinetta.

'I think he meant I shouldn't be hoity-toity about the job if I'd be happier doing it. And I would be happy. I loved that job, Vinetta. There's not been a day since when I haven't missed it. My mug'll still be there, my Port Vale mug.'

Vinetta still looked doubtful.

'Mother would like me to go back. I'd be making some money again. And I do hate sitting on the stairs brooding.'

Vinetta put her arm round his shoulder in a caring way. The two of them were sitting cosily in the kitchen. It was three o'clock on a bright but chilly afternoon. Out in the garden they could see Poopie pruning the roses whilst Wimpey was skipping vigorously on the crazy paving. From the breakfast room came the faint sound of music from Tulip's radio. The rest of the family were out of sight and out of hearing, each wherever they wanted to be, doing whatever they wanted to do.

'Nobody makes you sit on the stairs,' said Vinetta. 'You could sit anywhere in the house. You don't have to take any notice of your mother, you know. She doesn't mean everything she says.'

'It's not just that,' said Joshua. 'I like the routine, working at night, resting by day without feeling guilty.'

'Well,' said Vinetta, 'I suppose you're right. It's up to you. If it's what you want, then do it.'

Joshua gave a sigh of relief.

'I will. I will do it. I'm to start on Monday night. We'll get Appleby to write a note confirming that I'll be there.'

He turned the letter over and carefully read it again.

'Not a bad letter,' he muttered. 'Better than some we've had. Better than bombshells from Australia.'

They had not written back to Albert Pond and in the weeks since his last letter they had had no news of his coming. They began to hope that he would not come at all.

Mind you, they had still done a fair bit in preparation. The thick net curtains had been bought and put up at the windows. The light bulbs had all been changed. Joshua had his horn-rimmed spectacles ready and Vinetta had her blue-tinted ones. They were still waiting for a pair like bottle bottoms to hide Sir Magnus's jet-black eyes, but the optician had told Appleby that he would have a pair in two or three days' time.

Appleby was called down to write the reply and she actually volunteered to take it all the way to the office for him.

'Better than posting it,' she said in an unusually cheerful voice. 'You can't always trust the post to be on time.'

Her timing was very good.

'Here,' said her happy parent, fishing in his pocket. 'See if you can spend that.'

Appleby grabbed the three pound coins with a grin. She didn't go so far as to say thank you, but to have her looking bright and friendly made a pleasant change.

'I think she's improving,' said Joshua as his daughter left the room.

'Don't let her hear you!' said Vinetta. 'We've been hoping she'd improve for the past forty years. I feel sorry for her sometimes. She can't help what she is. None of us can.'

Joshua made his way to the stairs again as soon as Vinetta started to put clothes in the washing machine. He sat there for an hour and a half, not so much brooding as peacefully meditating. In his fist he held the old pipe that was naturally never lit, but that fitted so comfortably in the palm of his hand that it was a real aid to cogitation.

'Yes!' he said at last with pure delight. 'Of course! I won't be able to have a beard sewn on to my chin if I'm working. Nobody in their world can grow a beard overnight. Charlie might just happen to notice it. I couldn't take the risk.'

It was the perfect excuse. If there was one thing Joshua hated it was having a beard sewn on. It took ages to do, hair by hair, and it was far from comfortable. Kate had never intended him to be covered in whiskers. And it is best to leave things as they were meant to be.

15. Preparations

IN THE middle of March the weather changed to a lovely Spring of purple crocuses and brighter, generous days. It was almost possible to persuade oneself that Albert Pond would not arrive in April, that time at 5 Brocklehurst Grove could be induced to stand still. Googles lay in her pram on the back lawn for the first time that year. Her eyes shone and the sun gleamed on the perfect yellow curl that peeped out of her bonnet.

Poopie and Wimpey were taking turns sliding down the wooden chute. Vinetta was pruning the roses. Joshua, employed now and due to work that evening, was resting on the small sofa by the French window in the dining room. Even Tulip, at her desk in the breakfast room, had opened a window to let the air in. 'You'd never think it was just March,' she said to Appleby when the latter came in dressed in her new lightweight yellow anorak, all ready to go shopping.

'Soon it will be April,' said Appleby innocently.

'Too soon,' sighed her grandmother. 'I just wish to goodness it was all over with. I don't know what people want traipsing about the world. Why can't he stay where he belongs?'

'No use fretting, Granny,' said Appleby, perching herself on the edge of the breakfast-room table. 'If he comes, he comes. There's nothing we can do to stop him. Meantime, we have made quite a lot of preparations. I'm getting Granpa's spectacles today.'

'Take these to the post whilst you're out,' said Tulip, handing Appleby three letters ready stamped. 'And see if you can get a darker shade for my table lamp.'

'So Albert won't see you,' teased Appleby in a voice as near to mockery as she dared with her grandmother. There was just that little bit of extra emphasis on Albert's name, and omitting his surname sounded a shade too familiar.

The crystal eyes looked up at her sharply, but Tulip frowned and said no more. Appleby slid down from the table and looked in her purse.

'Granpa gave me ten pounds for his shopping but that might not be enough. Depends on how much Mr Sutton wants for the spectacles and how much the lampshade is. There are some other odds and ends too.'

Tulip looked at Appleby suspiciously, but took out her money box and handed over four one pound coins.

'You can settle up with your grandfather when you come back, but there's the money for the lampshade. And I'll want the change if there is any.'

Appleby made a face as she walked out of the room and she muttered, 'Mean old bag,' under her breath.

'Did I hear you say something, madam?' Tulip called after her.

'No, Gran, just cheerio. See you later. That's all.'

'It had better be.'

Out in the street, Appleby swung along the pavement in fair imitation of a fashion model on a very slick, quick catwalk. Her red hair was combed into a cascade at the crown, but on a lower level it lapped her cheeks and brow like thick pointed petals. She was wearing her favourite green-framed sunglasses. Under the yellow anorak, she had a white sweatshirt and a pair of dark tartan trousers. Her cloth hands were covered with candy-striped, fingerless gloves from which her small, well-shaped fingers stretched out to false pink fingernails. Over her shoulder she carried a large pigskin bag.

'Are the specs ready yet, Mr Sutton?' she asked the old optician who was sitting on a high stool behind the glass counter in his gloomy little shop.

'Yes, Appleby, m'dear. I managed to get you a nice pair from the wholesaler's rejects. Pebble glass and all. Just what you wanted, though I pity the actor who has to wear them. He'll not be able to see much.'

Mr Sutton bent down to the drawer beneath the showcase and drew out a brown suede pouch from which he took a pair of black-rimmed, thick spectacles whose owner had died before he could collect them. Mr Sutton did not mention this fact to Appleby. Such a nice lass, it was a pleasure to help her out.

'Perfect,' said Appleby. 'Just what we need for the play. How much do I owe you then?'

'Two pounds fifty will cover it,' said Mr Sutton.

'Are you sure?' asked Appleby, knowing perfectly well that the old man would not go back on this low price. It was a purely arbitrary amount.

Payment for the spectacles had already been made in advance by the deceased.

From the optician's, Appleby, dawdling now, made her way to the outdoor Market. There were lots of people there and it could have been a dangerous place, but Appleby had learned long ago that people at the Market were all too busy looking at things, things and more things, to pay any attention at all to passersby. The only possible difficulty was in dealing with stall-holders. There was a knack to it. If you were 'just looking' you must not be one of those customers who goes up to the stall and handles the goods. That would surely be asking for trouble. You must 'just look' from at least a yard away. Then, when there was something you wanted, you must plunge in, hold it at eye level to create an eclipse, and ask the price. If it happened to be too dear, you had to startle the stall-holder by holding it out to him, obliging him to take hold of it whilst you strode away and hurried off elsewhere. If the price was satisfactory, you would say quickly, 'I'll take it.' Then all the stall-holder was interested in was the money you slid out of your purse. He would be looking down at the merchandise, putting it in a bag, and the top of his head would speak earnestly to the top of yours. It took years of practice, but Appleby had had years of doing just that.

'This one,' she said abruptly, holding the deep yellow lampshade between herself and the swarthy stall-holder. 'How much?'

'Three pounds and forty pence only. Very reasonable.'

'I'll take it,' said Appleby. Money and goods were exchanged and neither party in the transaction could have provided anything like a satisfactory description of the other.

Next stop, the Post Office. Not the little Post Office where everyone knew everyone else. The big General Post Office with wooden railings to keep the queue filing round in order. From the stand in the corner where there were collectors' packets of foreign stamps for sale, Appleby dawdled to choose two large packets of assorted Commonwealth. Remembering how little she'd paid for the spectacles, she only hesitated briefly before picking out two more packs, Europe this time. Her interest in stamp-collecting was of long standing and perfectly genuine. She got Granpa's manuscript weighed and stamped. Then she posted Granny's letters.

*

Soobie, meanwhile, had spent the day in the attic. The sunlight filtered through the dusty skylight on to a jumble of unsorted, unsortable junk. Who had rocked in that ancient rocking chair? Who had once played with that white-painted doll's house? Where were their children's children now? A fire-screen, a broken-stringed guitar, a cardboard carton brimful of old hats, an oval mirror in a wooden frame, a sturdy round table on a single stem with carved claw feet, a footstool with a torn tapestry cushion, and among and between these distinguishable things, a host of undistinguishable objects, some semi-wrapped in scruffy paper.

Soobie's job, as he saw it, was to make the place slightly more habitable for the hours he and Googles and Miss Quigley might have to spend hiding there. There was Spring in the air and Soobie, truth to tell, felt like a bit of Spring-cleaning. A pile of old books with tooled spines caught his eye, but he disciplined himself to concentrate on the job in hand.

First of all he took an old piece of cloth and wiped the skylight, removing dust and cobwebs. The sun shone in more brightly. Then Soobie noticed for the first time that there was a floral printed curtain slung somewhat drunkenly right across the attic. Still sticking to his preconceived plan, he forebore to investigate and took one large, empty crate, a fortunate find, and began cramming as much small rubbish as he could into it, till between the round table and the rocking chair there was a space of cleared bare boards. If the rocking chair were well dusted and provided with a cushion or two from downstairs it would make a comfortable seat for Miss Quigley. He would manage with the footstool. Googles would be brought up in her carrycot. If she was upset, Miss Quigley could nurse her and rock her to sleep. Keeping Poopie quiet up there would be difficult, very difficult! He would have to go into the garden shed.

Next, Soobie rearranged the junk that could not be packed away into what he would call a 'tidy mess'. Within two hours the place began to look much more habitable. Then, and only then, did Soobie allow himself to lift the pile of books, about seven or eight in all, from their place in the corner on to the round table. There they would stay till the visitor arrived and Soobie would pass the time in looking at them by candlelight. He resisted the temptation even to read titles. Later,

later. Soobie made his own rules and kept them to the letter.

Now, he thought, when all that had been done, I will see what mess is hiding behind that curtain. He unhooked it from the rafter at the end furthest away from the outer wall. Then he let it fall to the floor. In the other half of the attic there was another skylight, still dirty, but the filtered sunshine picked out no mess, no rubble, just two very large wicker chests. This, Soobie thought, was not the normal way of things. The tidy room is not usually hidden behind the room full of rubbish. It is always the other way round. The rubbish might well have been hidden behind a curtain, with the other half of the attic available for use. Unless ... unless the chests themselves held some secret. His extensive reading made him wary of things hidden in chests in attics. He approached warily, preparing himself to be shocked or horrified.

The first chest he opened was a complete anticlimax. Bales of beautiful cloth vertically arranged so that any one of them could be easily drawn out and inspected. Soobie did just that and found himself looking at a familiar pattern that reminded him of Tulip. Vinetta would be delighted with this windfall. There would surely be enough cloth here to clothe them all twice over. He carefully replaced the bale he had removed.

The second chest was identical to the first. But when Soobie raised the lid he was startled to see, first of all, two pink legs wearing black patent leather shoes on their feet. Feeling just a little bit squeamish, he lifted them out carefully and put them on the floor. Next came two arms twined together. The hands were even better than his mother's – the finger joints had natural-looking lines across them and the fingernails were bedded in and did not look at all false. He laid them down very gently.

Next there was the headless torso. It was dressed in a Fair Isle patterned jumper, and roughly fastened round its middle was an unfinished short, grey pleated skirt. Soobie lifted the body very carefully. It had been lying on its front. When he turned it over he found pinned to its chest with a very large safety pin a label with the name 'Nuova Pilbeam' written neatly on it.

Poor, unfinished Nuova Pilbeam. It was an odd name, thought Soobie. No one in the family ever knew where his or her name came from, or even why the family name was Mennym. Yet each one had only one forename. If Nuova Pilbeam had been a Mennym she would have been the only one with two first names. Then he remembered that 'nuova' was Italian for 'new'. So this was, or would have been, the new member of his family, and if she had been finished her name would have been Pilbeam. A beautiful name! It was sad.

Some day, thought Soobie, I'll tell Mother about Pilbeam, but not now. Albert Pond was worry enough. Till he had been and gone again, other concerns would be suppressed. Thoughtfully, feeling the pity that was so much part of him, Soobie laid Pilbeam's body, arms and legs neatly on the floor beside the basket. Only the head was missing. With a shiver, but feeling unable to draw back, Soobie leant over the side of the basket and, looking down, he saw a bundle loosely wrapped in pale blue tissue paper. Using both hands widespread he lifted it out, handling it with the reverence due to something precious. Laying it on the floor, he proceeded to remove the wrappings. Soon he found himself gazing at a pale face with thick black braids either side of cheeks that each showed a spot of unnatural red. Pink lips that had never yet moved were stitched in fine satin thread in such a neat, compact blanket stitch that, in the attic light, they looked completely real. Arched black eyebrows surmounted long black eyelashes that swept upwards. Finer, lower lashes touched Pilbeam's painted cheeks. But where the eyes should have been there was a blank, unseeing space.

Soobie rummaged in the tissue paper till something pierced his finger. Looking down he found he was holding a brilliant black bead stuck on a metal pin stem. It was truly beautiful, lozenge-shaped, flecked with silver and with a deep, deep black centre to represent the pupil. Another bead, the same in every detail, was still lying in the paper. He held them both, one between each thumb and forefinger. Gazing down at Pilbeam's face, he suddenly knew what to do, a first promise, a step forward. He turned the pins towards the eyespaces and very deliberately pushed them into their centres. The face with its eyes complete looked much more real.

With melancholy respect, Soobie put the torso back into the chest with the arms and legs neatly by its side. Then he spread the blue tissue paper on top and laid Pilbeam's head on it. The black eyes seemed to look up at him, dazed and fearful.

'Don't,' cried Soobie with a sob in his throat. 'Don't worry. Sleep now. I'll come back for you some day when Albert Pond has gone.'

Then he closed the lid and tried to pretend to himself that he did not really hear a deep and troubled sigh.

Perhaps, thought Soobie, Mother will be able to finish her. But not yet. Soobie made his own rules and he stuck to them. Nothing could be allowed to come between the Mennyms and the visit of Albert Pond.

16. The Hi-jack

O N THE twenty-fifth of March, the family, with the usual exceptions, were sitting in front of the television set in the lounge watching the six o'clock news. Soon March would be April and the suspense was growing greater.

'*Scientists in California claim they have found evidence . . .*' the newsreader was saying. But no one was really listening. They hardly ever did.

'You'd have thought we'd have heard something by now,' Vinetta was saying, 'even if it was just a seaside postcard.'

'Perhaps he won't come after all,' said Soobie in a voice that sounded far from convincing. Then he went back to the book he was reading and took no further notice.

'Of course he'll come,' said Joshua irritably. 'He'll just arrive on the doorstep one day and then it will be panic stations.'

'*Reports are coming in of a hi-jack aboard a DC10 airliner en route from Australia via Cairo . . .*'

'What was that?' said Appleby, trying to draw attention to the latest news.

'Wimpey!' snapped Vinetta, 'stop drawing on your tights. Are you trying to make work for me?'

Wimpey was sitting right in front of the television set, her white-ribbed legs stretched out in front of her. She had drawn a happy face on one kneecap and was drawing a sad one on the other when Vinetta spotted what she was doing.

'*In Mainland China . . .*' droned the voice on the TV, passing to the next piece of news.

'Put that off,' said Granny Tulip, looking up from her knitting. 'It's always the same old thing, day after day, and nothing to do with us anyway. I don't know why we bother with television.'

Poopie, who had been playing with his Action Man in the far corner of the room, threaded his way through to the television set, knocking over Granny's wool basket and slyly thumping Wimpey on the way.

'*When we have any further news of the DC10 hi-jacking . . .*' The newsreader was stopped in mid-sentence as Poopie turned off the set.

'There,' he said frowning round at them all. 'Now we'll have a bit of peace.'

'Listen to him!' said Tulip in delight. 'Sounds just like his granpa. Children these days!'

Soobie, in his armchair by the window, looked up briefly from his book and slowly shook his head from side to side. He forebore to say, 'He's had forty years of practice.' But his expression said it for him, though only Joshua noticed.

'What if . . .' began Appleby in an unusually thoughtful voice. When she didn't finish, it was Tulip who snapped at her, 'What if what?'

'Oh, nothing,' said Appleby. 'It's silly. Nothing at all.'

'Suit yourself,' said Tulip going back to her knitting.

It was the family hour. Forty years of tradition put them all in one room at least till seven o'clock when the twins were sent to bed and everyone else was free to follow his or her own occupation. Joshua would set out for work. Tulip would go to her room and Vinetta would have her own private pretend in the kitchen.

A few days later, on the first of April to be precise, Joshua, coming home from work in the morning, picked up a letter from the mat inside the front door. An airmail. With a foreign stamp on it. A very thin letter. No weight at all.

He peered earnestly at the stamp but was none the wiser.

'Where's that fellow now?' he muttered to himself.

'Vinetta!' he called through to the kitchen. 'There's an airmail letter here. I wonder you haven't seen it?'

Vinetta came into the hall where the grand-father clock was fidgeting around to tell the world it was eight o'clock.

'Didn't hear the postman,' she said. 'Here. Give it to me.'

She took the letter and examined the outside thoroughly. The stamp was Egyptian. Date smudged. Envelope very thin. Might well have been empty. Carefully she shook it down and tore along one side. Then she opened it into a pouch and fished out a single, small thin sheet of pink paper.

'Oh dear!' she exclaimed as she read it. 'How awful for the poor man! He must have been terrified.'

Hearing Vinetta gasp and go on so, Tulip came hurrying from the breakfast room and even Soobie was curious enough to emerge from the lounge.

Tulip took the flimsy sheet from Vinetta's hands.

'Dear Family,' she read aloud to all of them. 'Written in haste. Hi-jackers have just released us from the plane in Cairo. Suppose you'll have heard about it on the news. Will write at length later. Still hoping to meet you. Sorry for the delay! Regards, Albert.'

'Poor boy,' said Tulip. 'What must he have gone through?'

'Still,' said Soobie with less sympathy and more practicality, 'at least he won't be coming here for a while longer.'

'If ever,' said Joshua hopefully. 'Maybe he'll just go back where he came from. I know I would if I were in his shoes.'

'Save that stamp for Appleby,' said Tulip. 'It'll go in the *All the World* album I bought for her last birthday.'

Appleby, of course, was still in bed.

17. Albert's Adventures

NOTHING was heard from Albert Pond till the middle of May. At first everyone had kept looking at the doormat expecting to see an airmail letter there any day. Poopie took to getting up early especially to see the postman arrive. He wanted to be first with the letter. He wanted to shout about it at the top of his voice and run upstairs with it to Granpa. That would show Appleby! But after a fortnight of vain expectation, the novelty wore off and they all went back to their normal routine.

When the letter did arrive it was actually Miss Quigley who spotted it. She had been paying a morning visit to the Mennyms: coffee and those delicious little biscuits, and how much better the weather has been, and how much nicer Appleby looks with her hair combed down, and how is Joshua doing now he's back at Sydenham's, and I really must be going now . . .

So, with not a little secret relief, Vinetta took her guest to the front door, ushering Miss Quigley ahead of her.

'Your postman's been,' said Miss Quigley, stooping down with surprising sprightliness to pick the letter off the mat and hand it to Vinetta. 'Airmail, I see,' she added.

Vinetta looked at the envelope. The stamp was Indian, definitely Indian. What on earth was Albert Pond up to now? Even Vinetta's rather patchy knowledge of geography told her that India was further away than Egypt. She hardly dared to let herself think what that might mean. It seemed too good to be true.

'And when will we be seeing you again, Hortensia?' asked Vinetta, holding the front door wide open, but calling Miss Quigley by her first name in an effort to show how friendly she was. 'Don't make it too long this time.'

Ever since the whole business of Albert Pond's visit had started, Miss Quigley had stayed away, brooding in her cupboard for weeks on end and then appearing briefly, pretending that she was so busy at her own little home in Trevethick Street that she just couldn't find time to come calling.

She didn't answer Vinetta's question directly. She just smiled uncertainly, eyed the letter with regret and apprehension, and made a swift departure from the front door with the barest of goodbyes. A few minutes later, when she glided silently in through the back door, she was looking very resentful and she even closed her cupboard door more loudly than usual.

Vinetta took the letter straight to the breakfast room. Joshua was lying down upstairs and she didn't want to disturb him. Sir Magnus, whom she had left in his bedroom with his desk on his lap and his pillows piled high behind him, would be sure to want to call a meeting and Vinetta couldn't face that yet. But she wanted to share the letter with someone, and Tulip was, after all, the handiest.

'On his way home by sea, I shouldn't wonder,' said the old lady, peering at the stamp. 'Not be in a hurry to get back in an aeroplane again after what he's been through. I know I wouldn't be.'

'Well, let's find out,' said Vinetta, growing impatient. The letter was quite bulky and very stiff.

Tulip took her pearl-handled paper knife and slit the envelope. Out fell several pages of paper and a photograph.

Vinetta picked up the photograph. It was a full-length picture of a girl who looked like a fashion model. She had long, golden hair and a big toothy smile. She was wearing a wide purple cape over a black outfit of which the most that could be seen was a pair of tight-fitting trousers and shoes with square gold buckles.

Vinetta turned the picture over. On the other side were scrawled the words This is *Hildegarde, taken at a fashion show in Paris.*

'Hildegarde,' mused Vinetta. 'Must be his girlfriend. And about time too!'

Tulip adjusted her spectacles and began to read the letter:

Dear Family,

So many things to tell you. Don't rightly know where to begin. At the end maybe. My Ma used to hate being kept waiting for the punchline to a story. I remember her now, when I'd come home from school with some tale or other saying, 'Get on with it, then. What's happened? Never mind the trimmings.'

So, getting on with it, let me tell you first and foremost, I am married. Not courting, not engaged. But honest to goodness married. There! I bet that took the wind out of your sails after all I said about having no intentions in that direction. Well, it was true at the time. And even now I scarce know what's hit me. But I do know that when I look at Hildegarde I feel like I am the happiest man alive. And all because of a hi-jacking!

I'll skip the terrifying bit. Though I don't mind telling you, it scared me stiff. Yet, you know, when you're one of a crowd and all you have to do is take orders, you become more dazed than anything else, like a zombie.

There was this girl in the seat next to mine and we settled for being terrified together. They told us not to speak. So we didn't. They told us not to move. So we stayed still. I don't mind admitting, I wouldn't be in line for a medal. In all fairness, though, it's not just a question of being brave in that sort of situation. No matter how brave I'd been, I still wouldn't have known what to do.

When it was all over and the terrorists had been persuaded to let us passengers leave, all I remember is stumbling across the runway at Cairo airport steering this beautiful girl by the arm. When we reached the airport lounge, she began to cry as if she'd never stop.

We had a drink or two and sat there waiting for what would happen next. Then suddenly Hildegarde, the girl I'm telling you about, said that nothing on this God's earth would get her back on any plane again. She's always been frightened of flying even though she's been all over the world as a fashion model. This last flight finally put the tin lid on it.

'I'm going home,' she said, holding my sleeve, 'and nothing, but nothing, will persuade me to leave Oz again as long as I live.'

So by the time I'd told her how I'd take care of her and we'd go home together by sea, we were just about engaged. It took a few days to get things organised, but eventually we got ourselves on to a cruise liner sailing to Australia down through the Indian Ocean. Just before we put in at Bombay, Hildegarde and I were married by the ship's captain.

Of course, you know what this means, don't you? Unless my dear wife (marvellous word that!) changes her mind, and I don't see that as being on the cards in the near future, I'll have to pass up my chance to visit the old country and meet my English family. Best we can do is keep in touch by mail. I've *put one of Hildegarde's fashion photos in with this letter so you can see the beautiful girl I've married. Perhaps you could send me a family photograph or two to let me see what you all look like. I can't tell you how disappointed I am that my visit had to be cancelled like this. Fate plays funny tricks. It obviously wasn't meant to be, as my Ma used to say.*

Still, if I hadn't planned to visit you all, if you hadn't encouraged me to come as you did, I might never have set out in the first place. Then Hildegarde and I would never have met. So I've got a lot to thank you for, putting me in the right place at the right time, though I don't mind admitting it didn't seem quite the right place when I was staring at the airplane floor thinking we were all going to be blown up any minute!

I've told my wife (there's that word again!) all about you and she too will be pleased to hear from you any time you can manage to drop us a line or two. We have some family visits to make after we land, but we expect to be home by the end of June.

Take care of yourselves.

Lots of Love,
Albert and Hildegarde Pond

'So it's over,' said Vinetta with relief. 'Let's tell them all. Let's tell them all now.'

There was no formal meeting in Granpa's room and no precedence as to who should be told first or last. The news was shouted round the house from top to bottom.

At three-thirty, after everyone had settled down again, Miss Quigley crept out of her cupboard and slyly put her gloves on the chair in the hall before going silently out past Vinetta who was busy pretending in the kitchen.

The front doorbell rang.

'I wonder who that can be,' said Vinetta, straightening her hair and making her way to the door still clutching the tea towel.

'Miss Quigley,' she said with a smile of welcome. 'This is a surprise.'

'I hope I'm not intruding, Vinetta my dear,' said the visitor. 'I think I must have left my gloves here this morning. Ah yes! There they are.' She gathered the gloves up from the hall chair and looked at Vinetta expectantly.

Vinetta took her cue.

'By the way, Hortensia,' she said. 'Remember that letter we got in the second post?'

'The airmail, you mean?' (As if there were any other.)

'Yes. Well, it was from Albert Pond. He's married and has gone back to Australia with his new wife. So he won't be paying us a visit after all.'

'What a pity!' said Miss Quigley. 'I've been telling my friends in Trevethick Street all about him. They were hoping to meet him. They'll think I've made it all up! Never mind! I'd best get along now, dear. My nephew is coming for tea.'

In the lounge, Soobie heard Miss Quigley's high, silly voice and winced.

18. Pilbeam

'WHERE is Appleby?' Soobie asked his mother one warm day at the beginning of June. It was an unusual question. Soobie did not normally show any interest in the whereabouts of his siblings. The twins and Googles were in the back garden with Tulip. Joshua was having his afternoon nap.

Vinetta was in the kitchen doing her favourite job. In a world of pretends, reals were very precious. Cooking was all pretend, and eating, and washing cups and saucers (except for every few months when they were freshened up to take the dust off them). But washing clothes and ironing were real. Washing, even with a modern washing machine, was not pleasant for a rag doll.

Damp clothes are, well, damp. The dampness from a bundle of washing could soak right through to the kapok. Washing, personal washing, was also necessary from time to time, but wet. No one really liked washing. It took such a long time to dry, especially if the sponge were a little too saturated and the water got right inside. But ironing! Ironing was warm and dry and joyful!

Vinetta stood the iron on its heel and looked at Soobie curiously.

'I'm not sure where she is, but she's not in the house. She went out about ten minutes ago, dressed for town and carrying her shoulder bag. Did you want her to get something for you?'

'No,' said Soobie. 'I just want to know that she is out of the way. She's too nosy and I have something special to show you.'

'Well, what is it?' asked Vinetta, pulling one of Joshua's shirts from the washing basket and spreading it out on the ironing board.

'You'll have to switch the iron off and come with me,' said Soobie.

'Well, where is it?'

'In the attic.'

Had it been anyone else in the family, except perhaps Joshua, Vinetta would have insisted upon knowing what she was going to see. She would have been very reluctant to leave a real to indulge someone else's pretend. But Soobie was different. Left to himself he did not have pretends. If there was something to be seen in the attic it would be real and it would not be trivial. Remembering Joshua's experience with the rat at Sydenham's, Vinetta shivered as she followed Soobie up the narrow, uncarpeted stairs that led to the attic.

When they went in, Vinetta was pleasantly surprised. In forty years she had seldom ventured into this unwanted space and, as she remembered it, it should have been dark, untidy and dirty. It was an alien area. Yet what she saw now was a very neat, huge, double room with two quite clean windows in the roof letting in broad shafts of sunlight. Near the door was a rocking chair and a single-stemmed round table. Junk there was too, of course, but orderly junk, tidily stacked and distributed. The other side of this enormous attic, beneath the second skylight, was empty except for two large basket-work chests. At the far end was another door, an architectural oddity, since there was no second staircase.

Soobie led his mother to the chest that held the bales of cloth. He threw open the lid.

'I found these whilst I was clearing the place ready for Albert Pond's visit,' he explained.

Vinetta drew out a length of cloth and tossed it on her arm till yards of it unwound. The sunlight from the roof illuminated a pattern of twining flowers in shades of red, brown and gold. Vinetta exclaimed at the beauty of the design and the quality of the material. Real stuff for another of her realities.

'I am a lucky woman,' she often said. Seeing this cloth made her feel very lucky indeed.

Soobie felt happy at seeing Vinetta so pleased, but, of course, there was more to be revealed. There was the other chest.

'What is in the other chest?' asked Vinetta. 'Surely not more material like this?'

'No,' said Soobie gently. 'There is something very surprising. I got quite a shock when I saw it.'

Vinetta looked alarmed and took a step back from the chest she had just been going to open.

'I don't like surprises, Soobie. I can do without surprises. Albert Pond was more than enough.'

'I know, Mother. But there is no way round it. It is certainly not a surprise I have deliberately prepared for you. It is just there, and it is surprising. It is not really terrible,' he went on, trying to reassure her. 'It is just that when Aunt Kate died she must have been in the middle of making something she had no time to finish.'

'Something?' queried Vinetta, fingering the lid of the chest.

'Someone,' said Soobie, correcting himself. 'There is a doll in there that needs to be put together. It is like us, but it is unfinished.'

Vinetta flung the lid open and looked down into the puzzled, sad black eyes of Nuova Pilbeam. She put one hand gently on the painted cheek. She lifted the head in its tissue paper and saw the body underneath, the name still pinned to its Fair Isle jumper, the sort that Appleby had worn in her bobbysoxer days. For some minutes, Vinetta stared without speaking and Soobie stood by her, silently waiting.

'Say nothing of this to any of the others,' said Vinetta at last. 'This is my business and nobody else's. Poor, poor Pilbeam!'

Carefully, with the eyes of a needlewoman, Vinetta examined every part of her unfinished child. Then she and Soobie tucked her back into the box and went down into the house heavy-hearted.

Appleby came home ten minutes after Vinetta had returned to the ironing board.

'Where have you been?' asked her mother.

'You'll never guess,' said Appleby in her usual irritating manner.

'Of course I won't,' said Vinetta crisply, 'and I don't intend to try.'

'All right, huffy! Well, I'll tell you anyway. I went to the booth in the station and had my photograph taken. I took eight of them altogether and I'm sending the best two to Albert Pond. I'll bet I look every bit as good as his Hildegarde.'

The photos were good. They showed a dazzling redhead in green-framed sunglasses wearing a black and green striped sweatshirt.

'They're lovely,' said Vinetta generously. 'I hope you'll be giving one to me. I can't see that it would do any harm sending a couple to Albert, but don't write too soon. Granpa thinks a very cautious and slow pen-friendship is probably what's needed to keep everything safe. Albert has his own interests now. He doesn't need us. He'll probably write two or three times. Then it will be just a card at Christmas, and eventually perhaps not even that.'

19. Appleby's Birthday

'HAPPY BIRTHDAY to you, happy birthday to you!
Happy birthday, dear Appleby,
Happy birthday to you!'

Tulip, Vinetta, Joshua and the twins sang in unison, Poopie managing to sound louder and flatter than all the rest put together. They were all in the dining room, a little-used room with highly polished dark furniture, a special occasion room. A dining table that could seat twelve people stretched from the doorway to the French window that faced onto the back garden. It was spread with a pure white linen cloth, deeply edged with fine lace, and on it were beautiful china plates pretending to be a feast. A few of the plates had some old sugary biscuits on them. The centrepiece was what looked like a real birthday cake, with candles and a frill round the edge and HAPPY BIRTHDAY APPLEBY written across the top. Against the longest wall was a high, ruggedly carved sideboard on which today was a pile of packages all ready to be opened by the birthday girl.

Appleby was proud of her birthday. Every fourth of July she reached the age of fifteen yet again. It was never clear at what stage of the year she reverted to being fourteen. Certainly at Christmas she was always fourteen. At other times she would be fifteen if being a little older gave her more prestige. Occasionally, in an argument, she might claim to be nearly sixteen. But the birthday always had to be her fifteenth.

No one else in the family ever had a birthday. The grown-ups were all too grown-up. Googles was only a few months old and her first birthday never came. The twins were ten at Christmas, every Christmas naturally, and that was part of the festive celebrations. Soobie could have laid claim to a sixteenth birthday, but he thought it stupid to pretend and wouldn't let it happen. He never came to Appleby's parties and no present from him was to be found in the pile on the sideboard.

'I'll open Granpa's present first,' said Appleby, tearing open the wrappings on the parcel labelled, with ornate flourishes, 'To my dearest granddaughter'. She always opened his present first, partly ritual, partly knowing that he usually bought the dearest for his dearest. This year it was a dark red leather writing case with a full set of pink, scented writing paper, envelopes and notelets inside. It fastened with a zip and had the initials 'A.M.' embossed in gold on one corner.

'I'll write to Albert Pond,' she exclaimed excitedly.

'I thought you might,' smiled Tulip, 'and you'd better open my present next.'

Appleby took the small oblong box her grandmother indicated. Inside was a stainless steel pen with 'Appleby' engraved on the side.

'It's a ball-point,' said Tulip quickly, 'but it's a good one. I hope you'll take care of it.'

'It's lovely, Granny,' said Appleby giving Tulip a quick hug before going on to the rest of her presents. Vinetta had given her an album for her fashion photos.

'It makes a change from stamp albums,' she explained. 'You must have dozens of them by now.'

Joshua gave his daughter a bronze elephant to add to her collection. Appleby was always collecting something and this had been the year of the elephant.

'That's ten I'll have now and this is the nicest. Look at its ears!'

The twins began to giggle when she came to their large parcel.

'The usual joke,' said Appleby with a grin, but began nevertheless to tackle the layer upon layer of paper that would be hiding a present of very small size and probably little value. Last year it had been a Mars Bar.

When she came to it at last it was even smaller and could easily have been thrown away with the wrappings. The twins waited eagerly for her reaction.

'Well, that settles it,' she said holding up a book of postage stamps. 'I really will write to Albert Pond. You couldn't have got me a nicer present.'

Poopie and Wimpey were delighted with their sister's approval.

'We went for it ourselves,' said Poopie. 'We got it out of the machine. It's not just the sort you buy at the counter.'

'We thought you might think it was silly,' said Wimpey, still a bit anxious, ''cos you're often at the Post Office yourself. Poopie said you might when I first suggested it.'

'Well, I don't think it's silly at all,' said Appleby sounding kind and quite grown-up. 'It's a lovely thought and a real encouragement. It goes well with the pen and the writing set.'

It was Appleby's day for being good and nice to everybody. They sat at the dining table and ate pretend cakes and sandwiches and drank pretend lemonade from real crystal tumblers. Then, finally, Appleby stood up, closed her eyes and made a wish as she pretended to blow out the fifteen unlit candles on the cardboard cake that Vinetta brought out and dusted year after year.

When the party was over, Appleby went upstairs to thank Granpa for his present.

'I'm going to write to Albert Pond,' she said, 'and I'm sending him those photographs I showed you.'

'Wait another week or two, my dear,' advised Granpa. 'You don't want to be too eager. If we get too friendly he might change his mind and come, wife or no wife.'

20. Pilbeam's Progress

THE ROCKING chair was rocking gently back and forward. All Soobie could see was the back of it as he stood in the attic doorway. Vinetta's voice was somewhere, reading a story he recognised about some children on a flying carpet looking for the end of the rainbow.

But where was Vinetta? And who was listening to this old tale?

It was late August and Soobie had felt a wish to see the attic again and have one more look at poor Pilbeam. So, after the family hour, he had given the twins time to settle down and then gone silently up the attic stairs. Even treading in soft blue slippers, it was not easy – the uncarpeted stairs creaked. The odd-shaped attic door, one side much longer than the other, lurched open, and Soobie saw that movement of the chair before he had even reached the top step. Moving nearer, he felt a shiver down his back as he saw the rockers lift and fall. Then he was reassured by the sound of Vinetta's voice reading the old familiar story.

He stepped right into the attic and, rounding the rocking chair that was still in motion, he came face to face with Vinetta who was seated on the footstool with the book on her knee. She looked up and smiled sadly and uncertainly at Soobie.

'Only you know anything of this,' she said, 'and that's how it must stay.'

Soobie turned away from his mother to look at the chair and its mysterious occupant.

Pilbeam was sitting there, smiling slightly but consciously and with black eyes that were taking on a look of intelligent interest. It was what Soobie had more than half expected. It was what he had wanted from the first time he had held the sorry little head in his hands. But that did not stop him from feeling amazed.

'Tell me about it, Mother. Tell me all about it. Tell me everything.'

Vinetta closed the book. Soobie knelt down on the floor beside her.

'I have spent my spare time for the last few weeks completing Pilbeam, fixing all her parts together into the whole person she is now. It has not been easy, but I knew it was possible. Remember your father's leg. No one would know that I had made it and not Aunt Kate. Time and time again I have mended Poopie and Wimpey when they have played too rough or fallen in the garden. This was more intricate, and it was difficult, but it was always possible. What I didn't know, and still don't know, is whether that poor child will ever come as fully to life as the rest of us.'

'She looks alive,' said Soobie. He looked at the girl still rocking in the chair. She was wearing a floppy pink sweatshirt, black trousers and a pair of trainers. 'I see you've changed her clothes,' he added.

'I couldn't leave her stuck in the style of forty years ago. If she is ever to join the family she must be on equal terms with other teenagers.'

'With Appleby,' nodded Soobie, giving a smile that was almost a grimace.

'Precisely.'

'So what happens next? What is there left to do?'

'She hasn't spoken yet. Till we get over that hurdle she cannot be said to be truly alive. That is why I talk to her and read to her whenever I can.'

Soobie picked up the book and looked at it affectionately but critically.

'She's too old for this sort of story.'

'I've thought about that,' said Vinetta, 'but it seems to me that when it comes to reading she has forty years of catching up to do. You like that book. I know you do. And she must be about your age. There is some part in each of us that is never too old for a good tale of magic. I do read other things – teenage magazines, murder mysteries, science fiction, newspaper articles. Soon I'm going to bring the portable television set up here, and perhaps we could have the old record-player.'

Soobie thought awhile. He looked at the book he still held in his hands.

'I have never read this book, you know. I was just born knowing that sometime in the non-existent past I must have read it. When I was about eleven years old – only I never have been eleven years old. Just thinking about it is a tremendous strain. How do we know what memories Pilbeam will be born with?'

'We don't,' said Vinetta. 'It is a new situation. We can only stumble on and do our best.'

Pilbeam was rocking a little harder and looking even more interested in all that was being said.

When Soobie turned to her, it seemed to him that she was a reluctant prisoner of silence.

'I'll help,' he said. 'I'll be another voice and I'll talk to her about music and plays and sport and all the things Appleby is interested in. How about movement? Can she walk?'

Vinetta shook her head.

'She can move, certainly. See how her hands grip the chair arms and make it rock, and she moves her head slightly as we speak, as if she were looking from one to the other. I have never seen her walk, but twice I have found her sitting on the floor in front of the rocking chair as if she had been making the effort but hadn't succeeded. It will take time, Soobie. It would be very surprising if it didn't.'

The two conspirators then discussed how they were going to take turns in looking after Pilbeam and coaxing her into life. By the time they had finished, it was growing dark.

'We should have a light in here,' said Soobie. 'I'll bring my torch up tomorrow. Candles would give more light, but they are risky at the best of times.'

'It might not be necessary,' said Vinetta. 'If you look at the beam that crosses the middle of the attic, you'll see that there's a fixture for a light bulb.'

'Even better,' said Soobie. 'All we have to do is find the switch. It's probably near the door. I'll fetch a bulb up tomorrow.'

The switch was actually outside the door. Soobie was pleased when he found it. The days would soon be shorter and a light would be needed to give them more time to work. There were, unfortunately, no sockets to be found, but the TV and the record-player were both able to work on batteries. This was a real job. Soobie took it very seriously. It was the first time he had ever been interested in anything that drew him away from his books and his chair by the window in the lounge.

21. Letters

IT WAS a very wet morning. Even the letters lying on the floor in the hall were damp. Tulip picked them up and scrutinised them. Only two letters this post – one a thin blue airmail addressed to Miss Appleby Mennym in the handwriting she immediately recognised as Albert Pond's, the other a very thick, long envelope with Sir Magnus's name on it. Tulip turned the thick letter over. On the back it said, 'If undelivered please return to Cromarty, Varley and Thynne, Solicitors . . .'

'Mmm!' said Tulip to herself. 'I wonder what that's about.'

At that moment, Appleby came down the stairs, still dressed in her dressing-gown, although it was eleven-thirty and the letters had come in the second post.

'Letter for you,' said Tulip curtly. She looked at her lazy granddaughter more closely. 'I might feel like asking you why you've still got your dressing-gown on at this time of day, madam, but, what's more to the point, why on earth are you wearing your jeans underneath it? Surely you haven't slept in them?'

Appleby snatched the letter.

'None of your business, but, as it happens, I was halfway dressed when I heard the postman and I thought there might be a letter for me. It is at least eight weeks since I wrote to Albert Pond and I knew he would be writing back some time soon.'

'If that is the way you talk to your grandmother, don't bother speaking again. It'll be a long time before I speak to you!' Tulip's crystal eyes glittered behind her little spectacles. She was very, very angry.

Appleby looked doubtful, even perhaps a little bit scared. As the years had gone by, she had grown more and more uppity, but it was not wise to have a big confrontation with Tulip. Even Appleby knew that.

'I'm sorry,' she said in a not very convincing voice. 'It is just that everybody is always on at me. I can't please any of you. You all think you can say what you like to me.'

'Very well,' said Tulip drily. 'Apology accepted. Now read your letter and let us know what Albert has to say this time.'

'What's that one?' asked Appleby looking at the bulky envelope Tulip was still holding in her hand.

'Letter for Granpa. I'm just going to take it up to him.'

She didn't bother to mention the solicitor and Appleby took no further interest. Her own letter was far more important. She tore open the envelope.

'Listen, Gran, listen!' she cried, forgetting her earlier animosity. 'Albert Pond wants me to pay them a visit in Australia. He says he'll send me the fare and I've just got to name the date when I can go. Isn't that marvellous?'

Vinetta came out of the kitchen to see what the excitement was about. Soobie swivelled round in his chair by the window and gazed in amazement through the lounge door at his dotty sister. Well, dotty was the only word he could think of at that moment to describe a rag doll who imagines that she could really take a trip to the antipodes.

'Appleby!' exclaimed her mother. 'What are you thinking of? You going there would be as bad as him coming here, worse if anything.'

Appleby looked crestfallen.

'I could have seen Ayers Rock, and Perth and Melbourne and the Sydney Opera House and the Harbour Bridge. It would have been incredibly wonderful. A dream come true.'

'None of our dreams come true,' called Soobie sourly from the lounge.

'You shut up,' snapped Appleby. 'Who asked you, anyway?'

Vinetta looked for a way to restore the peace. Even forty years' experience had not made her any less hurt by discord than she had been in the dim and distant past when her children had fought their very first fight.

'Perhaps we could pretend that you're going on holiday,' she suggested to Appleby. 'You could pack some bags and we could say goodbye to you at the front door.'

Appleby seized on this idea at once. 'And I could stay away for a month and you would all miss me, but I would send you postcards and I might even bring you some presents back.'

Soobie groaned.

'Where would you be for the month you weren't here, mutton head? In the cupboard with Miss Quigley?'

Vinetta and Tulip were scandalised. No one was ever supposed to mention the cupboard. Miss Quigley lived in Trevethick Street. Everybody knew that.

'Well,' said Soobie, coming out into the hall and looking shamefaced, 'she asks for it, going on the way she does. I'm sorry I said what I did. I shouldn't have.'

'I can stay in the attic,' snapped Appleby. 'Not that it's any concern of yours, Soobie Mennym.'

Vinetta was beginning to wish she had never mentioned a pretend holiday.

'You can't stay in the attic, dear. It is much too dusty,' she said quickly. 'Don't worry. We'll think of something.'

And there they left it for the time being. Tulip went off upstairs with the other letter, the letter for Sir Magnus. She had no idea that what she was carrying was a bombshell.

22. The Inner Circle

THERE was an emergency meeting of the senior members of the family in Sir Magnus's room that evening. The family hour was over. The younger children were in bed. Appleby was in her room. Soobie had made his way secretly to the attic.

Miss Quigley attended the meeting.

'She must come,' Sir Magnus had said firmly that afternoon. 'She has a right to be here. She's a silly woman and I can't abide her, but rights is rights!'

So Vinetta had gone, duster in hand, and given three quick, short taps at the cupboard door. Then she had immediately turned her back and started vigorously dusting the hall-stand.

The cupboard door opened behind her and Miss Quigley peeped out. Seeing Vinetta's back, she understood at once what it implied. So she waited and listened.

Vinetta called to Joshua, who was in the little cloakroom sorting out a pair of wellington boots for work, 'By the way, Josh, your father wants the Inner Circle to meet in his room at eight o'clock tonight. He knows you can't be there, of course, but I gather it is something important. I've sent a message to Miss Quigley inviting her to come along.'

The door to the hall cupboard closed silently.

Joshua had not heard what Vinetta was saying, but it wasn't really intended for his ears anyway.

'Why is it,' he was grumbling, 'that whenever it rains I have such a job finding my rain boots? There's tennis racquets, footballs and all sorts in here.'

At twenty minutes to eight that evening, Miss Quigley, carrying her grey umbrella, sped out through the kitchen to the back door. Two minutes later, there was a ringing at the front-door bell.

Vinetta hurried to answer it.

'You poor thing, having to come out on a night like this! I hope you've not got soaked. Let me take your umbrella. The fire's on in the lounge. Do come and get warm and dry.'

Vinetta fussed over her visitor. Miss Quigley was mollified but still anxious.

'I got your message,' she said as they went into the lounge. 'I knew it must be urgent. It's not that Albert Pond again, is it?'

Vinetta shook her head.

'I haven't the faintest idea what it is. Not even Tulip knows exactly. All we know is that he got a letter from a solicitor this morning and he's been in a mood ever since. It must be important. He said you had a right to be here. In fact, he insisted upon it.'

Miss Quigley looked quite flattered, but still tremulous.

Promptly at eight o'clock, the Inner Circle gathered in Granpa's room.

Sir Magnus was sitting up in bed, well propped up by pillows. The purple foot dangled listlessly. In his hands he held the letter.

'This letter,' he said, 'is from a firm of solicitors. They're not our solicitors. Strangers to me altogether. But I gather from what they have to say that we are now the owners of this house, or, at least, I am. There are various papers for me to sign and send back, but when the palaver's over, the house is mine.'

'That's wonderful!' exclaimed Vinetta. 'How generous of Albert! No more rent to pay! No more worrying about our future here!'

Yet Granpa did not look at all happy. He had not looked happy all day, come to think of it.

'There is a snag?' asked Tulip anxiously.

Miss Quigley, seated upright on the high-backed chair near the door, said helplessly, 'Perhaps the authorities will want to know more about us if you start signing things for strange solicitors.'

'I've spent too many years bamboozling bureaucratic incompetence for that to be a problem,' said Sir Magnus. 'Everything that needs doing can be done by telephone or by post. I've phoned my own solicitor already and he'll see to it. That is the least of my worries.'

'Well, what is troubling you then, Magnus? You're being very irritating. You've got the three of us very worried, and we don't know what we are worrying about,' protested Tulip.

'It is Albert Pond,' said her husband. 'He doesn't exist.'

'What on earth do you mean?' demanded Vinetta. 'Has he died?'

'No, I mean he doesn't exist. He has never existed. There is no such person as Albert Pond.'

The three women looked at him blankly.

'What makes you say that?' asked Vinetta.

'I know it is hard to believe,' said Granpa. 'It has taken me all afternoon to grasp it. But it must be true. I have been left this house in the will of Mr Chesney Loftus who died just three months ago in Australia. So if Chesney Loftus was alive a year ago when we first heard from Albert Pond, Albert Pond can't be real.'

'So this Albert, whoever he was or is, must be some sort of hoaxer,' said Vinetta, exploring the possibilities.

'A hoaxer who knows all about us?' Sir Magnus was directing them gradually towards the truth he had already deduced. 'I have spent hours trying to put the pieces together. The only conclusion I can come to is that this, in the parlance of detective stories, is an inside job. Albert Pond has to be one of us.'

'Us!' said the startled women, looking from one to another. It flitted through Miss Quigley's mind that she had been asked most particularly to be there. Surely she was not under suspicion!

'Well, not exactly us,' said Granpa, 'more likely, them!' He nodded grimly towards the door beyond which were the younger members of the family.

'Which one?' asked Miss Quigley, relieved of her momentary embarrassment.

'Well, not the twins,' said Granpa. 'Poopie might be capable of doing something like that out of pure mischief, but he is not clever enough.'

'So,' mused Vinetta, 'it would have to be either Appleby or Soobie.'

Granpa suddenly looked very, very old and very, very sad. The black button eyes had a film of grey. The white walrus whiskers drooped.

'It can only be Appleby,' he said. 'Even I have to see that. Soobie is too honest and straightforward. He never pretends anything. A monstrous pretence like this is beyond him.'

'But what about the letters?' faltered Vinetta, trying to grasp what the old man meant.

'She must have written them herself, disguising her handwriting. She is clever, you know. None of you realises how clever she is.'

'They were posted in Australia. You can't get away from that,' put in Miss Quigley.

'They had Australian stamps on them,' corrected Sir Magnus. 'That is another bit of evidence. Who is the stamp collector of this family? Who always goes to the Post Office?'

'The envelopes had proper postmarks,' Miss Quigley persisted, remembering the letter she had scrutinised as she handed it over to Vinetta.

'No problem for Appleby,' sighed Sir Magnus, shaking his head. 'Forgeries. Very good ones at that. I'm not saying they would have fooled Stanley Gibbons, but they were certainly authentic enough for us.'

'But the postman brought the letters. Appleby is always in bed when the postman comes,' objected Tulip.

Then Vinetta remembered, with a sinking feeling, the snowy morning when she had come across her guilty-looking daughter in the hall. Tulip thought about the jeans she had glimpsed under Appleby's dressing-gown just that morning.

'But what about the photograph of Hildegarde?' asked Miss Quigley. 'She showed me that the last time I came to tea.'

Vinetta looked grim.

'She's made fools of all of us,' she said. 'I should have known better. She has a shoebox full of fashion photos. I even bought her a photograph album for her birthday so that she could set them out nicely. She'll have been having a good laugh at the lot of us.'

Vinetta was furious, but at the same time she felt as if the bottom had dropped out of her world. She could not understand how a daughter of hers, well-loved to the point of being spoilt, could do such a thing. She had inflicted a year of agony on the whole family. It was beyond any understanding.

'What shall we do about it?' she asked, looking expectantly at her father-in-law.

'I don't know yet,' said Sir Magnus. 'You have the facts. I suggest we all think about it. Tell Joshua as soon as he comes in tomorrow morning. He'll be at home tomorrow night. So I suggest we have a full family conference tomorrow evening at seven o'clock. Maybe by then we'll have sorted something out.'

Miss Quigley looked a bit uncomfortable.

'Of course you must come too, Miss Quigley. My granddaughter, for whatever reason, has caused you a lot of worry and misery.'

Miss Quigley's prim mouth twitched. Her whole face looked crumpled. Then suddenly she stood up, looking taller and ramrod straight.

'I don't think I can go on pretending to live at Trevethick Street,' she said bitterly. 'I shall go back to my cupboard in the hall and sleep till I am wanted again.'

She turned and went out of the door and down the two flights of stairs to the hallway. Habit inclined her to turn left towards the front door, but with fierce determination she turned right and walked firmly along the passage to her cupboard. Tulip and Vinetta, looking over the banister, clearly saw her open the door and disappear inside.

'I wish she hadn't done that,' said Vinetta. 'It seems like the end of an era.'

Tulip felt much the same but she said briskly, 'Don't worry. She'll get over it. We all will. You'll see.'

'We could ask her to come and live with us properly. We have plenty of room after all,' suggested Vinetta feeling guilty.

'Oh, no we couldn't,' said Tulip. 'She would be unlivable with. I can take her in small doses, very small doses. And the same goes for the rest of the family. We have our rights too.'

23. Alone in the Attic

THE NEXT morning all of the grown-ups were subdued and anxious, determined not to say a word about Appleby's misconduct till the evening meeting. The four children were told simply to come to Granpa's room at seven o'clock. Their questions as to what it was about met with very vague replies. Even Soobie, who might have expected to be given an honest answer, was left in the dark.

Whilst the rest of the household was marking time, the girl in the attic took a huge step forward.

For weeks, Vinetta and Soobie had talked to her and guided her. They told her all about the family and its history, repeating things over and over again in different ways. They read to her.

They played all sorts of music on the little record-player. They pulled her wicker trunk over from the other side of the attic and put the portable television set on it. Being in the attic, reception was remarkably good. Her watching was always supervised, and when the guardians left the attic, the set was switched off. Both of them treated her like a very important, fragile invalid.

Pilbeam rocked in her chair and carefully watched everything around her. She learned how to smile and to frown. She had walked, yes walked, uncertainly from her chair to the round table. Vinetta had been delighted when she did this, but worried in case trying to do too much too soon might send her back to being inanimate.

But on the morning of the letters, nobody was with Pilbeam in the attic. The rain was pattering on the skylights. The day was dull and gloomy, the corners of the attic staying in complete darkness. Usually when she was alone like this, Pilbeam just rocked the chair from time to time and gazed rather vacantly at everything and nothing, wishing that Vinetta or Soobie would come. She had learned very rapidly how to wish.

This particular morning, however, was different. Pilbeam looked more intently around her, straining to see better. The pearl screen of the television was blank. The record-player was closed and silent. Suddenly Pilbeam made up her mind. Stiffly, but not as stiffly as she feared, she rose from her rocking chair and went to the door through which she had often heard Vinetta and Soobie enter behind her back. It was a funny little lopsided door, but Pilbeam did not know that. It was the only door she had ever seen. She found the knob and turned it. The door opened towards her. Somehow she knew, one of the things she was to discover she had been born knowing, that electric lights are operated by switches. So when she saw a switch on the wall outside, she pushed it down. And in the attic, suddenly there was light. Till that moment, the light had been a sort of magic trick worked by Vinetta and Soobie. Loving and considerate though they were, neither of them had ever thought of giving Pilbeam any light when she was alone.

Pilbeam stood in the doorway looking in at the well-lit attic and felt very pleased with herself. It was enough of an achievement for one day. The narrow, uncarpeted stairs did not call her yet. The rest of the house, for the present at least, could remain a mystery.

Pilbeam went back into her safe haven and shut the door. The electric light shone into every space. Moving more easily now, she began to explore. First, the books on the table. She took the top one and opened it. It was called *Pride and Prejudice*. Pilbeam, as one would expect of a sixteen-year-old, found that she knew how to read. It was yet another delightful thing that she had been born knowing.

So, for the next two hours, whilst a drama was quietly developing downstairs, Pilbeam spent her time getting to know the Bennets and their friends and relations. She stopped reading at the end of Chapter thirty-five, in which Darcy's letter to Elizabeth revealed the treachery of Mr Wickham. Downstairs in his room, at just that moment, Sir Magnus Mennym was pondering on the letter from Cromarty, Varley and Thynne, and coming to the unpleasant conclusion that there had been great treachery in his household and that the perpetrator could have been no one but his favourite grandchild.

Pilbeam, unaware of all this, became more aware of herself. She put the book back neatly on the pile and sat on the footstool, looking at her fingers and moving them systematically.

She got up and walked round the room, looking at this and that among the stacked-up junk. She made a conscious decision not to turn on the television set, although she felt sure she could have done so. The record-player looked more complicated.

In her rummaging, she came across the mirror. It was an oval mirror with a beaded wooden frame and it hung on a small matching stand. Pilbeam picked it up and went back with it to the rocking chair.

After one look in the glass, she spoke out loud her very first words.

'I hope she doesn't think I'll wear my hair like that! It looks awful,' she said sharply.

Being Pilbeam, and not Appleby, she didn't stamp her foot, or flounce, or throw the mirror across the room. Instead she put it gently on the floor beside her and began methodically to undo the braids that might have been all right forty years ago but most certainly weren't all right now.

When Soobie came up after the family hour, he was a little surprised to see the light on. He supposed that Vinetta must have been in and left it. The rocking chair was moving, but there was nothing unusual about that. He went into the attic and his first real intimation that something was different came when he bumped into the mirror on the floor and nearly tripped over. He turned quickly to look at Pilbeam. Her black hair was loose on her shoulders.

Before he could express any of the surprise and delight that he felt, the satin lips moved and Pilbeam said in a firm voice:

'I need a brush and comb. Go and get me one before Mother comes.'

Soobie was amazed. He stared at Pilbeam and didn't move.

'A brush and comb,' she repeated.

Soobie went on staring, speechless.

'How many times do I have to tell you, Soobie Mennym, I need a brush and comb? And I mean now, not next week.'

Hearing the tone of voice, Soobie groaned and said, 'Not another one!'

Pilbeam's black eyes flashed. She clearly had a quick understanding and an inborn knowledge of things and people that went far beyond what her tutors had told her. It was all falling into place at last. Human babies in their world have much less innate data to assemble and use, and much more time to do it in.

'Don't you dare say I'm like Appleby!' she cried. 'I don't spend my days making things up and pretending.'

'I'm pleased to hear it, Pilbeam,' said Soobie, 'but you could try being a bit more polite. Like say please.'

'All right! Please bring me a brush and comb. And don't tell Mother anything yet. I want to give her a surprise.'

'You'll do that, and no mistake!' said Soobie.

'The brush and comb,' insisted Pilbeam.

'Take it easy,' said Soobie. 'I'm going. I'm going. Don't be so impatient!'

As he went, Soobie's emotions were very mixed. He was staggered at what had happened. He was pleased. He was excited. But that did not stop him from feeling irritated by the rudeness of his new sister. And yet – he had to admit it to himself – if Pilbeam had been perfect, considerate and good-mannered, she would not have been a very convincing member of the Mennym menagerie.

And I suppose I'm no better than the rest of them, thought Soobie with his usual honesty, I sulk too much.

24. The Showdown

JOSHUA spent two hours talking earnestly to his father. On Tuesdays and Saturdays, a part-timer called Ernie Chubb looked after the welfare of Sydenham's property and premises. Like Joshua, he had been made redundant but later reinstated.

'Good job it's Saturday night,' Joshua mumbled. It was not exactly what he meant – he would really have much preferred to stay out of any family crisis, and this one seemed as if it might be unpleasant.

Sir Magnus, knowing his son's love of peace at any price, raised his bushy eyebrows and said sternly, 'You are her father. No matter what night it was you would have had to be here.'

'Not if it meant losing my job,' insisted Joshua. 'Remember what happened last time.'

And the last time, Appleby had written the note about his fictional illness. Appleby again! It always came back to Appleby.

'What matters more?' asked Sir Magnus grimly. 'Your job or your family?'

Joshua shrugged his shoulders.

'After all,' he said, 'no real harm's been done. We have the house. There is no Albert Pond. Appleby is what we have always known she was – a romancer.'

Sir Magnus looked exasperated.

'We have never known before that she was not just, as you put it, a "romancer", but a heartless, dangerous liar. I love her probably more than you do. I would rather forget about it. But she must be made to face up to what she's done for her own sake as well as ours. Until she does, unless she does, we'll never be able to trust her. We'll never know what she'll do next.'

They talked and talked, on and on. Joshua pretended to smoke his pipe. Sir Magnus pretended to sip his whisky.

'It's a strange world,' said the older man at length. 'We pretend to live and we live to pretend.

The rules are so complicated. Appleby just doesn't seem to know them.'

At seven o'clock prompt, the twins bounced into the silent bedroom. Joshua and Granpa had talked themselves to a standstill.

'What's the meeting about, Dad?' asked Poopie. It was exciting to be invited to another meeting. It was Granpa's meeting, in Granpa's room, but asking the head of the family was more than Poopie dared to do. 'Wait and see,' was Joshua's unsatisfactory reply.

So Poopie and Wimpey had to be content to go and sit down in their usual places on the ottoman. Wimpey, not to be outdone by Granny at the last meeting, had brought two large wooden knitting needles and a skein of red wool. Poopie had his double-jointed Action Man to play with.

Tulip came in next, carrying her workbasket. She made her way to the armchair and smiled affectionately at Wimpey. Then Soobie arrived with Miss Quigley, whom he had politely escorted from the cupboard. Appleby came in looking bright and breezy and totally innocent. Only Vinetta was missing.

'Where's your mother?' asked Sir Magnus, looking directly at Appleby who, as the latest arrival, might be expected to know.

'How should I know?' she said. Granpa looked furious and gripped his stick fiercely.

Soobie was surprised to see his grandfather looking so annoyed with Appleby, considering how often the old man had tolerated much worse cheek than that from his favourite grandchild. To smooth things over, the blue Mennym said carefully, 'I think Mother is in the attic. Shall I go and remind her?'

'She shouldn't need reminding,' growled Granpa. 'What's she doing in the attic anyway?'

'I think she's sorting out some material she found up there,' answered Soobie, not lying but slightly stretching the truth.

Just at that moment, Vinetta came in.

'I'm not late, am I?' she said, smiling apologetically at Granpa. 'I had to put the iron away.'

'In the attic?' asked her father-in-law in a sarcastic voice.

Vinetta flashed a look of annoyance at Soobie, but contented herself with saying, 'No. In the kitchen, of course. Now let us get on with this meeting.'

Nobody there had any doubt that a formal meeting was the right way of dealing with the problem. Whatever Granpa Mennym decreed was bound to be right because he was born old and very wise. All eyes turned to him as they waited for him to begin.

'This meeting,' he said portentously, 'is called to consider the behaviour of my granddaughter, Appleby.'

Appleby gasped and looked amazed and angry at the same time.

'My behaviour? What about my behaviour?' she snapped.

Granpa audibly cleared his throat. It was one of his most skilful pretends.

'We know all about Albert Pond,' he said, looking straight at Appleby. 'We know that he does not exist, has never existed, and that you, Appleby Mennym, made him up.'

Soobie gasped.

'Are you sure?' he said.

'Of course we're sure,' said Granpa, waving the solicitor's letter in the air. 'This proves it.'

Before Sir Magnus could explain everything to the younger members of the family, Appleby stood up. She had been sitting on a low stool at the bottom of Granpa's bed.

She gave them all a look of hatred.

'I'm not staying here to listen to this,' she shouted, and headed for the door.

Joshua put his hand out to bar her way.

'Let me go,' she screamed. 'I'm not staying here.'

She pushed her father's arm aside and bolted out of the room. They heard her run pell mell down the stairs and then out of the front door, crashing it behind her.

In Granpa's room, two floors above the street, there was silence for some seconds. Then Soobie said bitterly, 'Now you see where pretends can lead!'

'Shall I go after her?' asked Joshua doubtfully. Appleby had pushed him aside. He felt in duty bound to follow his angry daughter, but he was not sure what he would be able to say or do if he caught up with her.

It was Poopie who answered him. His yellow hair was all askew, his round eyes full of indignation.

'Let her go,' he said. 'She's just plain wicked. I don't care if I never see her again. She's horrible.'

Wimpey looked frightened. She loved her older sister. What is more, being a child herself, she thought Poopie meant the awful words he'd spoken. She worked herself up into a frenzy of worry.

'She will come back, won't she? She's not bad really,' she said, nearly sobbing. 'She's just naughty. I'm naughty sometimes. She gets mixed up, you see. Like me. I used to think there was a witch in the attic and I made up all sorts of stories about her, and I got really scared, but I never told anyone. And once I hid Soobie's shoes when he was in bed waiting for his suit to dry, 'cos I thought it would be funny to have him looking all over for them. Please, please, don't call Appleby wicked, Poopie. We need her back. She's our sister.'

The grown-ups let Wimpey ramble on. They all looked worried.

Miss Quigley summoned up courage at last to say awkwardly, but by way of comforting Vinetta, 'She'll come quietly in the back door and go to her room. It's the usual way. It will be better if nobody takes any notice.'

Vinetta gave her a grateful smile.

'Of course she will. And I think you should all let me sort things out more quietly with her when she does. Tell them about the house, Magnus, and how it is ours now. Then I think Poopie and Wimpey should go to bed. It is getting late.'

'I'll have to be going too,' said Miss Quigley. Returning to her pretend was the only way Miss Quigley felt she could be helpful. 'My little cat will be waiting for her supper.'

Vinetta understood at once and put her arm round Miss Quigley's shoulders. 'Everything all right in Trevethick Street, Hortensia?'

'Yes, thank you, Vinetta,' answered Miss Quigley bravely. 'You have no need to worry about me. Goodness knows, you have enough worries.'

When the meeting ended Miss Quigley went out of the front door, first retrieving her grey umbrella from the hallstand and putting it up as she stood on the doorstep.

'Try not to get upset, Vinetta,' she said gently. 'Appleby won't stay out long in this rain. If I see her, I'll tell her to hurry home.'

Miss Quigley took over an hour to make the journey for which she usually allowed herself no more than ten minutes. Braving the rain and the darkness, she went right to the gate and looked up and down the front street before going to check the whole of the garden and try, not very successfully, to see into the little window of the garden shed.

'The door's still padlocked anyway,' she said to herself. 'She cannot be in there.'

She walked round to the front of the house again and once more she looked up and down the empty street.

'I can't do any more,' she said at last. 'They really couldn't expect me to.'

So she went back to her cupboard feeling damp and downcast and disappointed. It would have been such a triumph to have brought the miscreant home. Though, in fairness to Miss Quigley, it must be said that her motives were not quite as simple as that. She was genuinely worried about Appleby, and really concerned at the anxiety Vinetta would be suffering.

25. Vinetta and Pilbeam

BEFORE THE meeting, Vinetta had, of course, been in the attic.

After Soobie had taken Pilbeam the brush and comb she so badly wanted, he had gone straight downstairs to find his mother. Vinetta, fortunately, was alone in the lounge, busy with a duster and spray can polishing the furniture. She was putting an unwarranted amount of energy into this activity because she was upset and angry. The object of her anger was sitting in her own room, two floors up, listening to pop music and fixing photographs in her album.

'Mother,' said Soobie, breaking into her thoughts and startling her, 'something very nice has happened.'

'That'll make a change,' said Vinetta drily.

Soobie knew that his mother had no love of surprises. That was why he kept his news as low key as he could. Pilbeam, Vinetta was told, had begun to talk. Pilbeam was moving round the attic better than ever. She had opened the attic door and switched on the light all by herself. Soobie did not mention his new sister's bad manners, nor did he tell her that Pilbeam had undone the braids in her hair. This bit of news he withheld so that Pilbeam could 'surprise' Vinetta in a less sensational way.

'I'll go up and see her now,' said Vinetta, glancing at the wooden clock on the mantelpiece. 'The meeting's not for another two hours.'

'Shall I come with you?' asked Soobie.

'No,' said his mother, 'I would rather go alone. If I am not down here in time, you could be kind enough to knock at the cupboard door and take Miss Quigley to the meeting. I think she would appreciate it.'

It was an unusual request. Soobie, not knowing about their visitor's decision to abandon Trevethick Street, was puzzled. But, being Soobie, he did not ask any questions and promised to do what his mother wished.

Vinetta put the polish and the duster away and then went straight upstairs. As she passed Granpa's room she heard him deep in conversation with her husband. Even in these trying circumstances, she felt pleased, for it wasn't often that the two men really talked to each other. She went very quietly up the final flight of stairs so as not to disturb them.

The attic door was ajar. Inside, Pilbeam was rocking her chair back and forward rhythmically, kicking the footstool with each foot alternately. She was singing:

> 'One two, the sky is blue,
> Three four five, I'm alive,
> Six seven, life is heaven,
> Eight nine ten, start again.'

And she did:

> 'One two, the sky is blue,
> Three four five . . .'

'Hello, Pilbeam,' Vinetta interrupted. 'You are doing well.'

Pilbeam stopped rocking and singing. She glared at Vinetta. Her black button eyes were well adapted to glaring.

'No prizes for who told you,' she said crossly. 'You would have been a lot more surprised if he hadn't. And I specially told him to say nothing. Just wait till he comes up here again. Some friend he is!'

In a way reminiscent of the grandfather she had not met yet, she kicked a small, round cushion with her left foot so that it spun across to the empty side of the attic.

Vinetta recognised this adolescent anger immediately. Forty years of Appleby was enough experience to turn anyone into a specialist.

'No need for that,' she said tartly. 'Soobie did tell me that you could talk now. He didn't tell me how cheeky you were, or I might have stayed away!'

Pilbeam was not Appleby. She was born knowing how to say sorry and to feel ashamed of her bouts of bad temper.

'I'm sorry,' she said in a genuine voice, 'but I did want you to be surprised and pleased, and he has spoilt it.'

'I am pleased,' smiled Vinetta, 'and a bit surprised too. I like the way you've done your hair. Soobie never mentioned that. It looks much better than those braids.'

'Do you think so?' asked Pilbeam eagerly, glancing at herself in the mirror.

'Yes, I do. You have lovely hair.'

'But Appleby has red hair. You told me she had. And she's pretty. Is her hair nicer than mine?'

'No,' said Vinetta, stroking the black hair affectionately. 'You both have lovely hair and I couldn't choose between you. Not that life is a beauty contest, though you might think so from some of your magazines.'

After that they sat down together, Vinetta in the rocking chair now and Pilbeam on the footstool, each doing her share of the talking. Vinetta gave all the news, even telling about Appleby's treacherous lies and the meeting that was going to take place that very evening to bring her to book. Pilbeam asked question after question.

'You could come down and meet everyone,' suggested Vinetta.

'No,' said Pilbeam, shutting up like a clam, so that the satin stitches on her pink lips began to look unreal. Vinetta looked anxious.

'I don't want you to live in the attic all the time and meet nobody. Miss Quigley's living in a cupboard is bad enough. There's a nice room downstairs next door to Appleby's.'

'No,' said Pilbeam again, and the satin lips closed firmly together so that Vinetta feared that it might be the last word she would ever say. She was very careful not to convey her fears to her new daughter.

'Is that all you can say?' she bantered as heartily as she could. 'I thought you liked talking now you've discovered how. I thought you were going to turn out to be a real chatterbox. Come on, what's the matter?'

Pilbeam relented a little.

'I'm not ready yet,' she said. 'Besides, I don't want to come downstairs till the trouble with Appleby's sorted out. What would she think if I appeared on the very day you all turn on her and face her with her wicked deeds? One way and another, I have waited forty years to become one of you, or so you tell me. A day or two longer, or even a week or two, is neither here nor there. I'm reading *Bleak House*. The time soon passes.'

'You're probably right,' sighed Vinetta, thinking with a sad heart of the coming confrontation. She looked down at her wristwatch.

'Goodness!' she exclaimed. 'Is that the time? I'm going to be late for the meeting!'

26. Sunday Morning

VINETTA did not sleep at all on Saturday night. She lay in the darkness, with her bedroom door ajar, straining to hear any sound. She thought Miss Quigley was right. Appleby should be allowed to creep back into the house and go to her own room without anybody noticing. But her mother desperately needed to know that she was there, and safe. So she lay awake and listened.

And she did hear sounds. Houses by night click and shuffle and groan from time to time. Sleepers turn in their beds But from midnight till dawn not a door opened, no foot was heard to tiptoe up the stairs. As usual, there was a dim light on the staircase and another in the hall. The darkness was relative not absolute. But no shadow crossed the shaft of light that shone in at the narrow opening in the door.

As soon as the palest daylight showed through the curtains, Vinetta crept from her bed, leaving Joshua blissfully sleeping as if nothing were wrong. She went up the short flight of stairs that led to Appleby's room and gently pushed the door open. The bed was still neatly made and unslept in. On the floor, Vinetta could just make out the shoebox full of photographs and the open album. Habit is strong. Vinetta was used to tidying up after everyone. She picked up the album and closed it carefully. Then she put both box and album on the desk by the window. That done, she sat down on the empty bed and sobbed.

'Perhaps she needs more time,' said Soobie's voice.

Vinetta, startled, looked up to see her son standing silhouetted in the doorway. With the hall light behind him, he looked tall and strong.

'Why did she do it, Soobie? Why?'

'Run away?' he queried, not sure what the question meant. 'I think she ran away because she was too proud to admit to all her lies. She is a very proud person. It would be very difficult for her to own up and say sorry for something so outrageous. She knows that.'

'That's not what I meant,' said his mother. 'Why did she tell all those lies in the first place? Why did she write those letters and make up all those stories about Albert Pond? It is still incredible to me that he doesn't exist. I almost wish he did.'

Soobie came into the dark room and sat in Appleby's basket chair.

'I don't know,' he said. 'I don't suppose we'll ever know. Perhaps she grew sick of shadows, like the Lady of Shalott. Maybe she is fed up with celebrating her fifteenth birthday over and over again. It could be her way of rebelling against being a rag doll.'

'I don't see why she should rebel. She gets everything she wants. She gets her own way all the time. I constantly make allowances for her immaturity.'

Soobie's blue face could not be seen clearly in the dull light of early morning, but it took on a look of controlled anger.

'She could resent that,' he said in tones as neutral as he could manage. 'After forty years she might prefer to be regarded as mature.'

'Then she should behave in a mature way,' said Vinetta sharply, appreciating all too well the undertones.

'Don't you see?' said Soobie more gently. 'That is the trouble, Mother. She can't. We are all caught in our own warp of time. She can never be other than adolescent.'

It was growing lighter. From the room below, Poopie's room, there came the sound of movements. Vinetta paused and listened before answering.

'You are only a year older than she is, Soobie. And you are mature enough. Even your grandfather says you have an old head on young shoulders. Why can't she be more like you?'

'I would say I'm different, but that is not fair. Everyone is different from everybody else. Kate must have had her own reasons for giving me a blue face. But here I am, the blue Mennym, who thinks too much. In my own way I am no more mature than Appleby. I haven't reached contentment with my lot. And I never will.'

Just then, Poopie came in and sat beside his mother on Appleby's bed. He was still dressed in his red striped pyjamas. His hair was more tousled than ever and he looked much younger than his ten years. He cuddled up beside Vinetta, looking for comfort in a strange situation, minding terribly the upset in his family.

A few moments later, Wimpey came in, still in her nightdress and carrying the American doll she got for Christmas.

'Would-you-like-a-Chocolate-Milk?' asked the doll.

Poopie, with the short memory of childhood, giggled, and then looked guilty. Vinetta sighed as she remembered Appleby chanting those very words last December.

Hearing the commotion, Tulip came from her own room and said briskly, 'Is this a private party, or can anybody join in?'

Vinetta smiled wanly and got up from the bed. She knew what Tulip meant and she knew that Tulip was right. Gathering together in Appleby's room could only lead to weeping and wailing, and that would do nobody any good.

'Go back to your own rooms, children,' she ordered. 'It's much too early for you to be out of bed.'

'Where's Appleby, Mother?' asked Wimpey. 'I came to look for her. Miss Quigley said she would come home.'

'I don't know where she is,' sighed Vinetta. 'I wish I did.'

The day was lighter now and the rain of the night before had mercifully stopped.

'She'll probably come back some time today,' said Soobie as hopefully as he could, but not really convinced by his own words. 'At least it isn't raining now.'

27. Sunday Night

IT WAS no ordinary Sunday. Every single pretend was abandoned. They did not gather to sit down at the white cloth and enjoy the illusion of a Sunday dinner. There would have been a space at the table and nobody could bear that.

In his bedroom, Granpa Magnus had no Sunday newspapers because Appleby was not there to fetch them. In front of him, on the portable desk, was a sheet of blank paper. He could not think of a thing to write.

'Can I get you anything?' asked Tulip three or four times in the space of half an hour.

'No,' Magnus kept answering absently. 'No. Thank you.'

Tulip turned her attention to the rest of the room. She opened the curtains a little wider. She straightened the lace runner on the dressing table. She moved her own armchair slightly to the left. She moved the ottoman a little closer to the door.

Magnus watched her, growing irritated, but when he spoke at last his voice was old and weary, not the irascible roar that usually expressed his irritations. Even his purple foot hung limp.

'Leave it, Tulip,' he said. 'Stop fussing with the furniture.'

'I wish she would come back,' said Tulip, getting to the heart of the matter. 'There's none of us will be able to settle to anything till she does.'

Miss Quigley's cupboard in the hall was high and narrow and empty except for the cane-seated chair on which she sat and slept. It was under the stairs, next to the much shorter, wedge-shaped cupboard where the meters were. At some stage in the house's history the two cupboards might well have been one. Was the cupboard made for Miss Quigley, or Miss Quigley for the cupboard?

On this Sunday, Miss Quigley sat on her cane-seated stiff-backed chair but she did not sleep. Instead she kept her ear close to the thinnest part of the door panel. Listening.

And hearing Poopie and Wimpey, who spent much of the day sitting on the bottom step of the staircase within sight of the front door.

'She might come in the back door,' said Wimpey at one stage.

'If she does, she'll still have to pass us to go upstairs, stupid,' said Poopie. His Action Man was hanging by a very long rope from the banister above. Wimpey had her knitting with her. The 'rope' was really a length of Wimpey's red wool. She had been induced to part with it when her brother explained that Hector, the Action Man, needed it to climb a mountain. To stop pretending altogether was impossible for the younger members of the family.

Joshua, Vinetta and Soobie spent most of their day in the lounge. For Soobie it was the natural place. If he had not been on the look-out for Appleby, he would still have been watching the world from the window. Not that there was much world to watch. The rain had stopped for the time being, but the sky was overcast and the air was raw. It was still just the beginning of October but it could as easily have been a December day.

Vinetta was sewing. Joshua was sitting still, looking uncomfortable, staring in front of him. He missed his pretend dinner and pretend tea and he longed for the comfort of holding his pipe and pretending to smoke. Joshua had very little imagination. His pretends were limited, but very durable.

'I'll have to get ready for work,' he said at last, relieved to see the clock on the mantelpiece tip him the wink.

'You're surely not going to work?' said Vinetta in angry tones. 'Not whilst Appleby is still missing?'

Joshua felt embarrassed but he stuck to his guns.

'I'm doing no good sitting here,' he insisted. 'Besides, I might see her on the street somewhere. I'll be looking all around me as I go. You can depend on that.'

'And if you meet her,' snapped Vinetta, 'What will you do? Tell her you can't stop or you'll be late for work? Ask her nicely to go home on her own?'

It was Joshua's turn to be angry.

'Of course I won't. What do you think I am? If I see her I'll be only too glad to fetch her home, work or no work.'

With that Vinetta had to be content.

It grew dark. Tulip drew the curtains in the big front bedroom and switched on the light. Sir Magnus was startled from a twilight reverie. He looked at Tulip intently for a few moments. She had stayed with him practically all day; knitting, accounts and breakfast-room business were all neglected. Whether to give sympathy or to seek comfort, her husband did not know – probably a little of both.

Suddenly Sir Magnus saw where he felt his duty lay. For the first time in forty years he swung round on the bed and put both purple feet to the floor.

'What are you doing?' asked a startled Tulip.

'I am going to look for my granddaughter. Nobody else seems to be bothering,' he answered with determination. He took hold of his stout stick and stood up. Then he walked stiffly, but holding himself admirably straight, to the wardrobe. In forty years he had never worn, nor even seen, his naval uniform. That wardrobe door had never been opened. But Magnus had been born knowing what was inside.

'Straighten the bed covers,' he ordered Tulip. She obeyed him instantly, but she still did not know what he was planning to do.

From the wardrobe he took the white uniform, with its gold braid and tasselled epaulettes, and laid it neatly across the bed.

'Now leave me,' he said and Tulip obediently went into the little room next door.

Sir Magnus was wearing one of his many nightshirts. He normally wore a fresh one at least twice a week. This particular nightshirt had broad grey and yellow stripes and reached down to the middle of his calves. All that could be seen beneath it was a pair of purple feet.

With a bit of a struggle, Magnus pulled on the dazzling white uniform trousers with the braces hanging from them. Then he removed the nightshirt and put on his dress-shirt, managing the buttons and the neck-tie as if he had done it all his life. There was quite a professional touch also in the way he flicked his braces into place. Next came the shoes and finally the jacket.

'You may come in now,' he called to Tulip.

He put on his peaked cap and pulled it well down over his black button eyes.

The sight took Tulip's breath away.

'I'm ready now,' said Magnus. 'I am going out there,' (he gestured towards the window in the manner of a great explorer) 'to seek and find the missing Appleby.'

'You can't walk down the street looking like that,' cried Tulip in a panic.

'And what is wrong with the way I look, madam?'

Sir Magnus surveyed himself proudly in the long wardrobe mirror.

'You look wonderful, Magnus,' said his wife. 'It is just that everyone will look at you. If you were flesh and blood dressed like that, they would look at you. It is dangerous. You look too . . .' she sought the right word ' . . . too magnificent.'

Sir Magnus sat down heavily on his bed. He felt exhausted. He was, after all, not a young man and his sedentary habits had not equipped him for strenuous exercise.

'Perhaps you are right,' he said, panting a little.

'I am,' said Tulip firmly.

'Leave me,' he said again, the white moustache quivering.

When Tulip was summoned to return half an hour later, Sir Magnus was back in bed, wearing his grey and yellow striped nightshirt, one purple foot dangling disconsolately from beneath the counterpane. The uniform was nowhere in sight.

*

Meanwhile, Soobie had seen the darkness creep across the front lawn and the raindrops begin to crowd on to the windowpanes. Joshua had gone to work, but Vinetta was still sitting with her sewing on her lap. She wasn't sewing now, just sitting, rocking slightly from side to side and looking intensely miserable. Soobie stood up and, without a word, he left the room. Vinetta barely noticed him go.

He went to the little cloakroom in the corner beside the front door. A pair of blue wellingtons was his first find. After some further searching, he found the dark blue, hooded coat that Vinetta had bought for him thirty years before. He had never worn it. He had never left the house. He had never intended to leave the house. But now, for his mother's sake, he had a job to do that made an excursion necessary. How he was going to do it he did not know, but he knew he would find out by trying.

'Where are you going?' asked Vinetta in amazement when he looked in again at the lounge. In his hand he was carrying a huge golf umbrella.

'I have come to tell you to stop worrying. I am going out to look for Appleby,' he said. Then he corrected himself. 'No,' he said, 'that's not right. I am going to find Appleby and bring her home.'

Vinetta, seeing the look of determination on her son's face, was torn between confidence in his ability to do what he said he would, and fear for one who had never before left the safety of the house. Her own expression betrayed her anxiety.

'Don't go too far,' she said, 'and don't stay away too long.'

'Don't worry,' said Soobie with a wry smile. 'I am the sensible, dependable Mennym. I'll keep calling home to tell you where I've been – that is if I don't find her within the first two hours or so. But, whatever happens, I'll go on looking till I find her. She won't be all that far away, you know.'

Vinetta went with him to the front door. The street was dark and deserted.

'Take care, Soobie,' she said anxiously. 'Are you sure you'll be all right?'

'Yes,' said her son. 'I will take care. I will be all right. Don't worry about me.'

He unfurled the umbrella and went out into the stormy, squally night.

28. Monday Morning

SOOBIE possessed great coolness of character. As he stepped out of the front door for the very first time he felt no fear and no trace of excitement. He was sixteen years old. This was his home town, and the mysterious memory with which he had been endowed made him instantly aware that he knew the place like the back of his hand. Turn right and you come to the High Street and the shops. Turn left and you pass three churches of different denominations before you reach the public park.

Soobie turned right. He could just visualise Appleby looking in shop windows or sheltering from the rain in some shop doorway. The shops were all closed, it being Sunday. Even the Bingo

Hall had put up its shutters at this late hour. At the far end of the street, the landlord of *The Black Swan* was locking up for the night, his last customers having departed ten minutes before. There were few cars on the wet road and not many pedestrians.

The first living being Soobie saw at close quarters, huddled in a shop doorway just as he imagined Appleby would be, was a very old woman sitting on a tiled shelf that projected from the shop window. She seemed to be wearing several layers of outer clothing. The hat on her head was tied on with a scarf. She was wearing a pair of men's boots and very thick stockings. At either side of her was a very large bag, each crammed full of goodness knows what, perhaps all her earthly goods. Soobie peered at her cautiously under the rim of the golf umbrella. His hood was pulled well down. The old woman looked up at the umbrella and grinned, showing a mouthful of broken teeth.

Soobie moved quickly on. Towards the end of the street, on the opposite side to the public house, he saw a group of teenagers clustered together in an arcade. The careful blue Mennym crossed the road before he could come within range of their interest. He sensed their potential hostility.

The rain was getting heavier. It came down noisily on his umbrella. It bounded up from the puddles on the pavement and spattered the hem of his coat. Time passed, but Soobie walked on and on, keeping close to the shop windows.

On the corner of one of the side-streets, he spotted a telephone box. Being sixteen, he knew perfectly well how to use it. Self-analysis would have been unbearably confusing. He had to accept that there were many things he was born knowing. And the habits of forty years had not made it a difficult thing to do. Being naturally provident, he had thought to bring some money out with him.

'Hello, Mother,' he said when they were connected. 'I'm in a phone box just off the High Street. It is two o'clock now. I'm just ringing to let you know not to worry about me. I've seen no sign of her yet, but I'm going on looking.'

'How wet are you?' asked his mother anxiously.

'Not so bad,' replied Soobie. 'My boots are waterproof, you know, and the umbrella takes care of the rest of me.'

He omitted to mention the trickles of water that managed to run hither and thither about his person, wetting his arms up to the elbow, and the front of his neck where his coat fastened. The hood was not a perfect fit.

'Try to get some sleep, Mother. I won't ring again till after four unless I have some definite news.'

He continued his search, up and down one side street after another, pausing, peering, almost willing his sister to appear. One street looked a real possibility. It was full of specialist boutiques and the clothes in the windows looked very like Appleby's. But apart from a black kitten mewing in a doorway, the whole street was empty.

Once he really thought he saw his sister at the very bottom of a street. He hurried down it as fast as he could. Fortunately, the girl was standing still, sheltering under an overhanging shop front. Otherwise Soobie, plump as he was and not very quick on his feet, would never have got near enough to establish that this was just another human teenager. From a distance she looked strikingly like Appleby. Soobie thought that only his runaway sister would be out on the streets at that time in the morning, but after he had seen a few more waifs and strays, he began to appreciate that Appleby was not the only youngster spending the night away from home. The others, thank goodness, were not his worry.

'Hello, Mother,' he said when he came back to the telephone box again. 'It is half past four now. I've searched the town centre from one end to the other. I thought for sure she would be around here somewhere, but she's not.'

'Come home then,' said Vinetta. 'Come straight home now and get dried off. You can't tell me you've managed to stay dry in this weather, no matter how good your umbrella is.'

'I'm not too wet,' said Soobie, shivering, 'just a little bit uncomfortable. If it gets too bad I will come home. But there's a street leading past the Market Place and down to the river that I'd like to look at. You know how much Appleby likes the Market.'

The Market Place was bare. Iron rails marked off where the stalls would be set up on market days. Wet rubbish clung round the railings. There were food cartons and old newspapers and plastic carrier bags waiting to be swept up in the early hours of the morning. The whole place looked bleak and sordid. There was no sign of life. No Appleby. Not even a stray cat or dog ventured into the open on a night like this.

Soobie, losing all hope, still persevered down the steep, cobbled street that led to the riverside.

Tall grey buildings either side were mostly in darkness. Street lamps of an old-fashioned style had very half-hearted pools of light surrounding them so that between one lamp and the next there were areas of blackness.

For the first time, Soobie felt fear. It was not a fear of anything external or rational. It was a fear bedded in the spirit, the great inner being that Mennyms, who knows how, shared in common with humankind.

I am nobody, he thought, going nowhere. Appleby might no longer exist. The rest of the Mennyms might have ceased to be and I might even now be all alone in the world.

It was not a pretend; it was a grasping after some awful reality. Soobie kept on walking towards the riverside. He came within sight of the great cantilever bridge that spanned it and he stood still in the middle of a mean, dead street to think.

At that moment a fog-horn sounded, solemn and mournful.

But to Soobie it was like the fingers of a hypnotist snapping to waken him out of a trance. Very deliberately, he folded up his fear and tucked it away in the back of his mind.

'I am going to find Appleby,' he said out loud, 'no matter how hard it is, or how long it takes.'

He was suddenly aware that the night would soon be ending. A daylight search would be impossible for a Mennym with a blue face, even if he hid as well as he could within his ill-fitting hood. And what is more, the umbrella would soon look extremely conspicuous, for the rain was stopping again.

'I'm coming home now, Mother,' said Soobie when he reached the telephone box again. 'It will soon be too light for me to be out. If she doesn't come back today, I'll try again as soon as it is dark.'

When Soobie reached home, Tulip and Vinetta were waiting at the door for him. They fussed over him as if he too had been among the missing. The umbrella was taken from him and put into the cloakroom sink to dry. He automatically wiped his feet on the doormat but then he was led into the lounge before he could remove his coat.

Vinetta undid the buttons and Tulip tugged off one sleeve at a time, as if he were no older than Poopie. His grandmother felt the coat between her fingers and said, 'It's very damp. We knew it would be. I'll put it to dry.'

Vinetta made him sit down in his usual chair and she pulled off his blue wellingtons. The gas fire was on full.

'Stay there till you're properly dried out,' she ordered, 'and then go to your room and have a lie down. You shouldn't have stayed out so long.'

Half an hour later, Joshua came home. He took off his damp coat in the hall, put his umbrella beside Soobie's in the wash basin, and changed out of his rain boots into his indoor shoes. Nobody helped him. But then, he had only been to work. He hadn't spent the night searching for his daughter.

'Any word yet?' he asked Soobie as he sat himself down at the fire in the lounge.

Soobie did not answer. He had fallen fast asleep.

29. Monday Afternoon

GRANNY Tulip was in the breakfast room trying to work out a rather complicated knitting pattern. She had made up her mind that if she worked hard at this problem, Appleby would be home before she had finished. It was pure self-comforting superstition, like not stepping on the cracks in the pavement. But it was a way of diverting the mind from an unbearable sorrow.

At midday, Vinetta looked in. She was wearing her dark green coat with the velvet collar turned up. Her brown fur hat and blue-tinted spectacles completed her cover-up against the outside world.

'I'm going out, Mother,' she said. 'I'll be back by five o'clock. Could you keep an eye on the twins? Don't let them disturb Soobie or Joshua. They're both lying down.'

Tulip put her knitting pattern to one side and looked at Vinetta shrewdly.

'It'll be like looking for a needle in a haystack,' she said. 'You are wasting time and energy.'

'I have shopping to do,' said Vinetta defensively. 'I want to buy Soobie some new gloves.'

'And since when does shopping take you five hours? Come on, Vinetta, admit it. You are going to search the town for Appleby. I don't blame you, but I think it is labour in vain. She'll come back herself when she is good and ready.'

'I will go all around the town,' said Vinetta stubbornly, 'not in the hope that I will find her, but that she might see me passing by wherever she is hiding, and that might give her the chance to come out without seeming to climb down. I am trying to meet her halfway, wherever halfway may be.'

Tulip picked up the knitting pattern.

'Go on then,' she said. 'I'll work in the lounge till you come back. But, for goodness' sake, don't pin your hopes on finding her. If she doesn't want to be found, she won't be.'

And she didn't, and she wasn't. At five o'clock precisely Vinetta arrived home again, weary and defeated. Poopie and Wimpey met her on the doorstep.

'We've been very good,' said Wimpey. 'Granny played cards with us and then when it got to half past four we all sat looking out of the window to see you coming.'

'I saw you first,' claimed Poopie.

'No, you didn't,' said Wimpey. 'We all saw you at the same time.'

Tulip looked at the stricken face of her daughter-in-law and said sharply to the children, 'Stop arguing. Can't you see your mother's worn out?'

Vinetta took off her outdoor things and went to sit by the fire in the lounge. Tulip retired gratefully to the breakfast room. Keeping the twins quiet was no easy task! Vinetta by now was too tired to try; so it was fortunate that Poopie and Wimpey decided to go their separate ways – they were definitely best apart.

Poopie went to his own room and started making an assault course for his Action Man, complete with scaling tower, jungle path and log bridge. He had accumulated a quantity of genuine equipment given as presents, but he was also very good at improvising with cardboard boxes, coathangers and scatter cushions. Once he had decided on turning his whole room into an area for manoeuvres, the problem of entertaining him was mercifully solved for a week or more.

Wimpey did not stay long in her room. She looked out of the window but there was nothing to see. It was nearly dark and the window in any case faced out on to the back garden. It occurred to her that Appleby might be hiding in the shed, but she was too timid to go out at this hour to find out. Then she wondered if anyone had thought of checking the empty rooms in the house.

On the ground floor there were no unused rooms. The kitchen, the little conservatory, the breakfast room, the playroom, the day nursery, the lounge, the dining room and the cloakroom were all liable to be looked into at any time by any member of the family. They were not good hiding places.

On the first floor, there were four bedrooms, a bathroom and a large airing cupboard. Poopie and Wimpey had rooms facing each other. Their parents' room, with its adjoining night nursery, was next to Poopie's. The bathroom was next to Wimpey's room, and on her other side was a 'guest' room, used only once in forty years by Miss Quigley on a disastrous weekend visit.

Tiptoeing past the room where Joshua was sleeping, and past Poopie's door that was not quite shut, Wimpey went to check the guest room.

In the gloom, she made out the neatness of a bed that had not been slept in and chairs that were still in their mathematically correct positions. The mirror on the small dressing table by the window reflected the light from the landing. Wimpey did not need to go any further to find that there was no one there. She briefly checked the bathroom and the big airing cupboard. Then, having resolved to make a thorough search, she headed up the staircase to the floor above.

There were four bedrooms, a bathroom and another large airing cupboard on this floor too. In the airing cupboard below, where the hot water tank was, Vinetta kept all the sheets and blankets. In this airing cupboard there was a cluster of hot and cold water pipes going from top to bottom, and two slatted shelves. It was nearly always empty and tended to collect cobwebs. Wimpey looked in cautiously and then, satisfied, quickly shut the door again.

This bathroom and airing cupboard were at the top of the stairs at the end of the landing, facing Soobie's room. Wimpey crept past just as Soobie was beginning to wake up. Next came the big front bedroom occupied by Granpa Mennym. Off it led the little dressing room where Granny kept a truckle bed for her own use. This small room had, of course, no door on to the landing. Across the landing from Granpa's room was Appleby's. Next to that was another guest room, slightly smaller than the one downstairs, but pleasanter. Wimpey headed hopefully for this second guest room but it too was neat and tidy and totally unoccupied.

A few feet further on was the narrow, uncarpeted staircase that led to the dreaded attic. Braving herself to make a journey she had never made before, Wimpey started to climb the creaky stairs.

Suddenly the attic door swung open. Wimpey, who had been looking without really expecting to find, was so startled she fell backwards onto the carpet at the foot of the stairs.

'I've found her,' she yelled. 'Come quickly, Mum. She's up in the attic.'

30. Wimpey Meets Pilbeam

THE ATTIC door had swung inwards and the light from the bulb on the rafters shone out on to the landing. Just as Wimpey fell and shouted, Pilbeam came out on to the top of the stairs, her stairs. She was little more than a silhouette with the light behind her, but not Appleby's silhouette, taller and sleeker with long straight hair that looked decidedly black. Wimpey, gazing upwards, saw immediately that this was a stranger.

'It's not Appleby,' she screamed, and promptly fainted.

From Granpa's room came the sound of a stick being vigorously thumped on the floor. He had no intention of leaving his bed again unless there was a fire. Once was more than enough! Someone would have to come and tell him what was happening.

Soobie, almost ready for his evening search, came out of his room to investigate the commotion. Seeing Wimpey lying still at the bottom of the attic stairs he dashed forward just as Pilbeam was making her way down to see what she could do for the child she had just scared half to death. Pilbeam, reaching her first, stooped and took her in her arms.

'Get Mother,' she said urgently to Soobie. 'I'll look after Wimpey till you come back.'

Pilbeam had recognised Wimpey immediately. No one else in the house could so exactly have answered the description Vinetta had given of her.

Soobie, after no more than a second's doubt, raced off to find his mother. Sir Magnus was still thumping on the floor with his stick. Soobie put his head round the door and said sharply, 'It's all right, Granpa. Just the twins again.' A plausible explanation.

As Soobie passed his parents' bedroom on the floor below, Joshua, almost ready for work, looked out to see what the fuss was about.

'Has she come back?' he asked Soobie.

'No,' said Soobie. 'Where's Mother?'

'Downstairs, I suppose,' answered Joshua and he went back into his room and shut the door. He was well used to the noise of his boisterous family and, once satisfied that Appleby was not the source of it, he lost interest.

Poopie did not even hear the noise. His assault course was getting along famously and he was unaware of anything else that was happening.

In the lounge, Vinetta was sitting with Googles on her knee, singing a bit chokily, 'Hush a bye, baby, on the tree top, when the wind blows the cradle will rock . . .'

Googles was not settling down comfortably. One little hand was tugging at the beads around Vinetta's neck. The little legs were stretched out rigid in an effort to reach the floor. Vinetta stopped singing and sighed.

'Poor little Googles. I have been neglecting you. All this worry about Appleby is upsetting our routines.'

Just then, Soobie came rushing in. 'Put Googles back in her cot, Mum. Wimpey has found Pilbeam and she's in a state of shock. You'll have to come.'

Googles was placed in the carrycot and immediately she began to cry loudly and vigorously.

Fortunately, Tulip, who had been working in the breakfast room, came out to see what the row was about.

'Take care of Googles, Mother,' said Vinetta hastily. 'She is very fractious today. I have never known her to be so naughty. And I really must go and see to Wimpey.'

'What's wrong with Wimpey?' asked Granny Tulip anxiously, but she still picked Googles up from the cot and began to shush her.

'She's had a fall,' said Soobie, 'but don't worry. It's nothing serious. She's just looking for attention. She'll be all right.'

Soobie and Vinetta dashed up the two flights of stairs to the upper landing. When they got there, they found Pilbeam sitting on the bottom step of the attic stairs nursing Wimpey who was just coming round and still looked dazed.

'Let's all go up to the attic,' said Vinetta. It seemed the best place to be in the circumstances. She took Wimpey by the hand and led the way.

Wimpey looked back over her shoulder at Pilbeam.

'Who is she?' she asked in a whisper.

'Just wait,' was her mother's short reply as she took her into the attic.

'But who is she?' persisted Wimpey, raising her voice now and looking all around her at the attic furnishings, Soobie's record-player, the spare TV set.

Pilbeam sat down on the footstool as soon as she came in. She said nothing. Vinetta sat Wimpey on top of the wicker chest, the one with the bales of cloth in it. Both chests had been pulled well forward and formed a boundary between Pilbeam's part of the attic and a huge stretch of emptiness beyond. On the other chest, the television set was making a vain attempt to get people to listen to the news.

'Turn that off,' said Vinetta as she sat down in the rocking chair. Soobie did so and then sat himself on a couple of cushions on the floor.

'Well! Who is she?' demanded Wimpey loudly and, for good measure, she kicked her heels against the side of the wicker chest.

Pilbeam glowered at her. An unconscious Wimpey might appeal to Pilbeam's maternal instincts; an objectionable brat, sitting on her wicker chest and talking as if its owner were not present, most certainly did not.

'This is Pilbeam,' said Vinetta. 'When Appleby comes home, we are going to bring her down to meet the family. She is going to live with us. She doesn't want to come down yet and we are keeping her a secret.'

'A sort of surprise,' said Wimpey excitedly. 'But where did you get her from?'

Pilbeam glowered more than ever.

'Well,' said Vinetta. 'I have been thinking about that. We can pretend that she is your cousin from Canada and that she has come to live with us because she has always wanted to come to England.'

'No, you won't,' cried Pilbeam indignantly, jumping to her feet. 'You'll do no such thing. You are my mother. Soobie, though I am sorry to say it, considering what a sneak he is, is my twin. Appleby, Wimpey, Googles and Poopie are my younger sisters and brother. So there!'

The lips were definitely not perceptibly pink satin any more. They had become highly mobile and now expressed all the anger and determination Pilbeam was feeling.

Vinetta was at a loss what to say.

'But where have you been?' insisted Wimpey. 'Why have we never seen you before?'

'I've worked that one out for myself,' replied Pilbeam. 'It was not easy. There were so many things I was born knowing and then Soobie and Mother told me so many more things, things I seemed to know already. But I have had time to think these last few weeks. And I have worked it all out. I've been here in the attic all the time. Aunt Kate died before she could finish me. So I lay asleep till Soobie and Mother found me and brought me to life. That is the truth and it is better than a load of rubbish about Canadian cousins.'

She did not know and would never know that she had been found totally dismembered.

Vinetta looked ashamed of herself. She got up from the rocking chair and put her arms around her daughter.

'You're perfectly right, my dear. The truth is always better. It is just that we are so used to pretending. It's a habit hard to break.'

'You've been asleep in the attic ever since Aunt Kate died?' asked Wimpey in wonder, trying to get it straight in her mind.

'Yes,' said Pilbeam simply.

'But that was forty years ago. You've been asleep for forty years. It's like the Sleeping Beauty.'

'What shall we do now?' asked Vinetta. 'Will you come and meet the rest of the family?'

Like her twin, Soobie, so like him in many ways, Pilbeam made her own rules and she stuck to them rigidly.

'No,' she said, 'I am staying here till Appleby returns.'

She turned to Wimpey quite savagely. Gripping her narrow little shoulders, she stared into the baby blue eyes and said sharply, 'Don't come back here till you are asked. And don't tell anyone else in the house, not even Poopie, that you have seen me. Understood?'

'Yes, Pilbeam,' said Wimpey, the pale blue beads flickering nervously. 'I'll not tell a single soul. Honest.'

Fear need not have come into it. Wimpey was quite prepared to worship Pilbeam, and Pilbeam was ready and willing to accept her young sister as an adoring acolyte. Still, there was no harm in being on the safe side.

31. Searching Again

VINETTA returned to the lounge leaving an excited Wimpey to settle down in her bedroom. There would be no family hour this evening. Poopie did not need telling. He was so busy on manoeuvres that had he been wanted downstairs someone would have had to go and fetch him. Tulip was already in the lounge, sitting by the carrycot where Googles was now sleeping.

'I'll take her into the nursery,' said Vinetta.

'She took some pacifying, I can tell you,' said Tulip, keeping her voice down. 'You'd think she knew there was something wrong.'

Vinetta smiled sadly but said no more. She carried the cot next door and returned immediately to her chair beside the fire. Joshua came in as usual to spend a little time with the family before going to work.

'Where is everybody?' he asked.

'In their own rooms,' replied Vinetta without bothering to explain why. Joshua was always content with simple answers. Long explanations were boring and unnecessary.

'No news?' he asked.

'None,' said Vinetta.

There was a short silence.

Tulip switched on the television, to give some background noise. And they all sat there, ignoring it.

Joshua gave a cautious look at his wife and his mother, then took out his pipe and cradled it in his hand. When is a pretend not a pretend? He needed to smoke the unlit pipe.

The weather forecast was saying that there would be more heavy rain in some part or other of the British Isles.

And there was.

'Listen to that rain,' said Joshua, going to the window and lifting the curtain to look out. 'It's on with the boots and out with the brolly again!'

He got up and went to sort out his wet weather clothing.

'I'll be away now,' he called from the hall after a few minutes.

'Bye,' answered the two women.

Tulip switched off the television, and went to the breakfast room, peeping in at the sleeping Googles as she passed.

Vinetta did not move. She listened to the rain on the windows and she grew more and more intensely miserable. The agony of wondering where her daughter could be on a night like this felt like a fist in the stomach taking her breath away.

'Oh, Appleby,' she groaned, 'where, oh where, are you?'

But it was Soobie who answered her. He was there at the lounge door, dressed in the hooded coat again and the blue wellington boots. In his hand was the golf umbrella.

'I'll find her, Mother. I will find her. She's wilful but she is strong and resourceful. I think I know where to look.'

This time when he went out into the stormy night he did not turn towards the town and the well-lit shops. He turned left, past the first church which was closed up and in complete darkness, on to the second church which was dimly lit but still closed. He walked right up to the arched doorway of this second church and looked carefully in the corners of the porch. A little boy of about nine or ten was sitting in a huddle with his knees up to his chin. But there was no sign of Appleby.

The third church had two entrances. A large double door in the centre of the front facade was firmly shut. Soobie even tried the metal ring that formed the handle. It looked promising. There were lights in the stained-glass windows. There was a definite air of a building that was not closed and shuttered. Soobie looked along to the right and his eye fell on the second door. It was smaller, no bigger than an ordinary house door, and narrow and, what was more to the point, a little bit ajar.

Cautiously, Soobie went in. He found himself in an inner porch where there were noticeboards on the walls, and two coat stands. Looking through the glass partition into the nave, he saw that there were three or four individuals sitting, or kneeling in silent prayer, well separated from one another, very private people in a very private place.

He watched for a while before slipping quietly into the far end of the back pew. He knelt before the statue of a lady with a child in her arms. Appleby was not there, but the prayerful mood of the place gave him another straw to clutch at.

In deep shadow he pushed his hood back just far enough to make it clear that he knew to bare his head in church. Being Soobie, always honest to himself, he was prepared to be no less than honest to God.

'I do not know who made the part of me that thinks. I do not know who I really am or what I really am. I am never satisfied to pretend. I cannot pretend that you are listening to me. I can only give you the benefit of the doubt. And it is a massive doubt, I can tell you. I do not know whether I believe in you, and, what is worse, you might not believe in me. But I need help and there is nowhere else to turn. The flesh-and-blood people who come here have something they call faith. Please, if you are listening to a rag doll with a blue face, let the faith of those others be enough for you to help me. I must find my sister, or my mother will be the first of us to die. Dear God, I don't even know what that means!'

It was all he could say. After he had said it, two things came to his mind. First, he knew now just why he had to find Appleby. Secondly, he had the feeling, and it was no more than a feeling, that someone somewhere had heard his prayer.

He went out into the wet autumn evening and wandered in the direction of the park. The gates were closed, but times being what they were, the railings by the gate had been vandalised and there was a gap of ample size for even Soobie to pass through.

He wandered down the broad path till he came to a junction. To the left a narrower path led upwards among some tall leafless trees. To the right the broad path continued downwards past a grassy playground to the lake. Weak, old-fashioned lamps lit both paths and were reflected in the rainwater. The rain was still falling, thin but steady. Soobie's coat was soaked. It was fortunate that the blue wellingtons were more waterproof than the old golf umbrella.

He stood at the junction for a few seconds. Then he decided to follow the more sheltered, narrow path up among the trees. After a few yards, he passed a park-bench and then another one. They were arranged at intervals all along the path facing, through the trees, the green, the playground and the more distant lake.

Soobie walked slowly and bleakly on. At the top of a walk that came up from the lake and split the green into two large areas there was a wooden building, all shuttered, with what looked like the face of a clock just perceptible through the darkness in a little lantern tower. Soobie kept on walking towards it.

Just before he reached the building, on the last seat, he saw what looked like a very large bundle of dirty rags. Soobie knew at once that it was Appleby, for no other reason than that for the past ten minutes or more he had expected to find her there. Some instinct had told him that she would be lying just as she was, scruffy and desperate, not knowing where to turn.

Soobie was pleased to find her. He was overjoyed to find her. But he didn't show it.

He went up to the seat and grabbed her wet arm.

'Come on,' he said. 'You're coming home. Your mother's worried sick.'

Appleby looked up at him wildly. Still defiant, she made herself say, 'So what?'

Soobie bit his blue lip and was about to say something salutary when Appleby's defiance suddenly crumbled and she slumped back on the seat and sobbed.

There was nothing more to say. Soobie took her by the arm and, without a word, supported her wet weight along the path, through the gap in the railings, and out into the dark street.

32. Appleby Takes a Bath

IT WAS ten o'clock in the evening when Soobie struggled through the front door supporting Appleby, who was leaning on him like a dead weight. His coat was wet, his umbrella was torn and his boots were covered in mud. But his discomforts were nothing compared to Appleby's.

Tulip and Vinetta had rushed together to answer the doorbell. They brought the wanderers in out of the cold, rainy night into the comfortably heated hall. Soobie quickly removed his wet coat and dirty boots and put his ruined umbrella in the cloakroom.

Then they all concentrated upon Appleby. Her beautiful red hair was matted with mud and looked no colour at all. Her sweatshirt and jeans were caked with dirt. She had somehow managed to lose her shoes and her socks were in shreds. Her green eyes looked unseeing and lustreless. They were obviously nothing but green buttons, sewn in place by Kate forty years ago. Whatever magic had turned them into functioning eyes had gone. Only the mouth remained alive, turned down at the edges and quivering.

Vinetta looked shocked. All the things she might have said, the reproaches she might have made, the explanations she might have demanded, remained unspoken. When Appleby slumped forward, Vinetta caught her in her arms and hugged her tight till the murky water that had penetrated her whole body began to ooze out. Tulip and Soobie helped to take her into the lounge and they laid her down on the settee.

The mouth still quivered but nothing else moved.

'What shall we do?' Vinetta asked Tulip, looking terrified.

Tulip looked at her filthy granddaughter and her distraught daughter-in-law.

'She will have to have a bath in one of the big baths,' she said decisively. 'All that dirt has gone deep into her system. Sponging or even showering will not get it out.'

The green buttons flickered to life for a moment. Appleby looked horrified. But she had not the strength to protest, or even to maintain her look of horror for long.

Vinetta was worried. No one had ever had a bath. A sponge down, yes. Even a very quick dive into and out of the shower. But a bath?

'Are you sure, Tulip?' she asked doubtfully. 'The water will go right through her. We'll never be able to get her dry again.'

Tulip's crystal eyes looked hard and determined, like a doctor who knows his insistence upon drastic surgery is risky but right.

'There is water inside her now,' she explained, '– filthy water. She looks to me as if she's fallen into a pond. We must get the dirt out and then think about how to dry her afterwards.'

On the settee, Appleby lay stretched out and lifeless. Dirty water was dripping from every part of her. Her face, hands, and all of her clothing were covered in slime. Bits of green weed were clinging to her. She looked not just wet but drowned.

'There is no life left in her,' said Vinetta as she timidly touched her daughter's arm. 'It would be cruel to put her to any more torment. Let her rest.'

'No,' insisted Tulip, 'we must be cruel to be kind. There will never be life in her till she is clean and dry. If she is allowed to dry off in the state she is in now, she will dry stiff and solid and goodness knows what problems that would lead to.'

'How do we know that she'll ever come to life again?' asked Vinetta, but even as she asked it she remembered the head, limbs and torso they had found in the attic. They had become Pilbeam, and Pilbeam was as alive as any of them.

'We don't know,' replied Granny Tulip brusquely, 'but we have nothing to lose by trying.'

Soobie had stood by silent, considering what was said. Then he put his weight behind his grandmother's wisdom.

'We'll have to carry her up to the bathroom on the first floor. We can fill the bath with warm water and put some shampoo into it. Whatever we wash dries. Our hair dries. Our clothes dry. So though it may take longer and be more difficult, you can depend on it, Appleby will dry.'

She was heavy. My goodness, she was heavy! They lugged her up the stairs and into the bathroom. They sat her on a chair whilst the bath was being prepared. Soobie, having helped with the heavy work, left his mother and grandmother to get on with the business of washing.

Since every bit of Appleby was made of cloth, it did not occur to them to remove the dirty sweatshirt and jeans. Only the tattered socks were pulled off ready to throw in the rubbish. When the bath was felt to be of a suitable depth and temperature, Appleby was plunged into it. The soapy water soon turned black and scummy.

Vinetta fetched a scrubbing brush from the kitchen and scrubbed away at her daughter's hair, face, arms, jeans, sweatshirt, everything. After half an hour, Appleby was, if possible, wetter than at first, her body soaking up the water like a sponge, but she was not much cleaner.

'Pull out the plug,' ordered Tulip, trying to stay calm, but by no means sure that the remedy she had prescribed was going to work.

The dirty water drained away leaving a broad, black tide-mark round the bath, and slumped inside it, a dazed, grey figure making feeble efforts to move arms and legs.

'She's still moving,' said Tulip, feeling frightened but trying to sound hopeful.

'What next?' asked Vinetta with a tinge of anger in her voice.

They tried to lift Appleby out of the bath, but she was too heavy.

'Get Soobie,' ordered Tulip. 'We'll take her to the bathroom upstairs and run another bath, but before we put her into it, we'll rinse the dirty suds off under the shower up there.'

Soobie, Vinetta and Tulip dragged Appleby up the next flight of stairs, over the beautiful blue Durham carpet.

'The carpet's getting filthy,' said Soobie.

'Never mind the carpet,' snapped Vinetta. 'That's easily seen to.' She was almost out of breath and fully out of patience.

As the suds were washed away under the shower, Appleby began to look a normal colour again. Her face was turning pinkish. Her hair was back to its natural shade of red. The green sweatshirt was still streaked with dirt, but recognisably green. The jeans were nearly clean and Appleby's feet and ankles showed beneath in flesh-coloured hues with toe-nails painted red, though the paint was chipped and the toes were still greyish.

'She has toe-nails!' exclaimed Tulip, and then on closer inspection, she added, in a voice of disapproval, 'and she paints them!'

Appleby still could not speak but she gave her grandmother a withering look as much as to say, 'They're my toe-nails and I'll do what I like with them.'

'Into the bath with you,' said Tulip as she and Vinetta tipped her into the clean water. This time the suds did not go grey and the scrubbing brush stayed white. After a final ducking under the shower, Appleby looked almost normal.

Almost, but not quite. Her limbs and torso, full of water, looked bloated. Her cheeks were abnormally plump so that the green button eyes were almost lost in their folds. She was dazed. Her movements, oh yes she was still moving, were slow and laboured. She looked like a spaceman. She still could not speak.

'Soobie,' said Tulip, 'go and take the shelves out of the empty airing cupboard.'

Soobie went next door and quickly removed all the slats that formed the two shelves and stacked them in a corner on the landing.

In the meantime, Vinetta and Tulip together, using four very large bath-towels, dried Appleby's hair and squeezed as much water as they could out of her limbs. Soon the towels were saturated, but, except for her hair, Appleby looked just as wet as ever.

'Now,' said Tulip when Soobie returned, 'fetch Appleby's basket chair from her room, and another couple of bath-towels from downstairs. Put the towels on the airing cupboard floor and the chair on top of them.'

By now, they had the terrified Appleby sitting on the bathroom stool, one either side supporting her. When Soobie had done his job, he helped the two women to manoeuvre his sister into the chair in the cupboard. Tulip explained to the dazed girl what was happening.

'You can sit here in the warm till you dry out. Go to sleep. No one will disturb you. It may take a week or two, but you must get completely dry. That is all you have to do. We'll look in on you from time to time to see how you are doing. I'll bring you my little brass bell. If you want anything, you can ring it.'

Oh, there were levels upon levels to that speech! Practical it was, and helpful. But Tulip was really putting on the biggest pretend of her life. She was pretending desperately that this bizarre situation was just a bit of ordinary, everyday life.

And at another level, she had a quiet, malicious satisfaction in thinking that this adolescent, who had caused so much trouble, would be stuck in a cupboard for a considerable time to think over her misdeeds.

'You will be all right?' asked Vinetta diffidently, longing to take Appleby in her arms and make it all better there and then, but knowing that such instant relief was beyond reach.

Appleby gave her mother a look of cool resignation. The pretend had just about worked. She could almost believe that, given time, everything might be all right. And, to be truthful, she was longing for them to close the door and leave her to recover, or even to die, alone.

33. The Last Conference

IN THE darkness, Tulip slipped quietly past her sleeping husband into the dressing room and changed into clean, dry clothes. Sitting in front of her mirror, with only the low light burning, she methodically adjusted her face and her hair till she looked her usual unruffled self. The damp, dirty clothing was hidden in her washing basket. No trace of the tussle remained.

On the floor below, Vinetta was cleaning the bath where Appleby had left so much dirt.

In the hall cupboard, Miss Quigley shifted uncomfortably on her cane-backed chair and felt aware that things were happening in the house at a time when things should not be happening.

Poopie was fast asleep, impervious to everything, even the Action Man making a lump in his pillow.

Wimpey heard noises in the dark, felt afraid, and covered her head completely with her quilt.

In her cot in the night nursery, the best baby ever invented was quietly sucking her thumb. Few and far between were the nights when Googles failed to sleep.

Joshua, of course, was still at work, sitting in his office and trying to make sense of all sorts of odd ideas. Forty years of utter simplicity had left him ill prepared for all the complications of recent months. He half-wished that Vinetta had left him in ignorance of that other matter. There was just too much to worry about. His hands, cupped round the Port Vale mug, gripped it tightly as if he were trying to hold on to some last vestige of reality.

Tulip went and sat on the edge of the bed where Magnus still slept.

'Magnus,' she said softly but urgently, 'wake up. Wake up.'

Her husband groaned and eased himself forward on his pillows.

'What is it now?' he asked in a less than friendly voice.

'It's Appleby,' answered Tulip. 'She's come back. Soobie found her.'

Sir Magnus came fully awake at those words and sat bolt upright.

'Where is she? Bring her here. I want to see her,' he demanded, pulling the cord that switched on the ceiling light.

Tulip looked uncomfortable, a sixty-five-year-old child caught out in being exceptionally naughty. If only she could blame Vinetta!

'You can't see her yet,' she said in an unusually timid voice. Then she gripped her husband's large hand tightly and made up her mind to tell the whole truth.

'I've done something dreadful, Magnus,' she blurted out. 'I thought it was for the best at the time, but now I don't know what's going to happen. I might have killed her.'

She told him all about bathing Appleby and getting her so wet that she looked as if she might never dry out. She did not blame anybody else but admitted freely that the idea had been hers.

Sir Magnus watched her, fascinated, as she told the story. When she described how bloated with water Appleby was, it was all he could do to stop himself saying, 'How could you be so stupid?

Why didn't you at least take her clothes off first?' But he held his peace.

'I think now,' went on Tulip, 'that it might have helped if we had taken her clothes off first, but I just didn't think. At the time, it seemed important to be quick and thorough.'

Sir Magnus was so used to Tulip running everything, seeing to everything, paying all the bills, being the most efficient member of the household, that he found himself feeling more kindly to her in failure than he had felt for many years. He was born knowing they had been childhood sweethearts, but that was something else.

'We all make mistakes,' he said gently, holding her little hand in his. 'Besides, Vinetta was there. She could have stopped you. But it's done now. There's no use crying over spilt milk.'

Tulip gave a sigh of relief. The problem was no better, of course, but she felt somehow absolved of her guilt.

'Do the others know that Appleby is back?' was Magnus's next question.

'They're in bed asleep.'

'Get them up and bring them here. Miss Quigley too,' said Magnus.

'At this time?' queried Tulip. The clock on the wall said twenty to three.

'The time doesn't matter,' her husband replied. 'Appleby is back and they're entitled to know. Besides, we will have to make it clear that they are to stay away from our airing cupboard.'

The Trevethick Street visitor ritual was omitted. Tulip knocked at the cupboard door and when Miss Quigley opened it she said abruptly, 'We're all to go to Sir Magnus's room straightaway. It's important.'

The twins were excited at being wakened up at such an odd hour and needed no second telling.

Vinetta by now had changed into her nightclothes and came hurrying up in her dressing-gown with Googles in her arms.

Only Soobie failed to attend. First of all he ignored Tulip's knock.

Vinetta tried.

'Granpa wants us all there,' she said loudly, after Soobie had failed to respond to two heavy raps on the door.

'Well, I'm not coming,' he growled at last. 'I'm tired out. What does he think I am?'

Vinetta then noticed the pile of blue clothing in a heap just to the left of his door. That was proof against any further pleading. The clothes would have to be washed, dried, aired and ironed, before Soobie would leave his bed again.

'He should really have another set of clothes,' sighed Vinetta. 'One set isn't enough for anybody.'

Granpa had wanted personally to praise his grandson as the hero of the hour, but he had to be content with giving him his due *in absentia*.

'So,' concluded Sir Magnus, looking emphatically at the sleepy twins sitting on the ottoman in an unusual state of truce, 'we will all have to stay away from that airing cupboard. In fact, if you have no business on this landing, don't come upstairs at all.'

Suddenly, out of the blue, the end became a beginning. Just as they were about to leave and go quietly back to their beds, Wimpey piped up.

'Does Pilbeam know?' she asked innocently, and then bit her lip and gave a frightened look towards her mother.

'And who, may I ask, is Pilbeam?' asked Granpa Mennym.

Vinetta made up her mind.

'I think it is time you all knew about Pilbeam. It is a sort of miracle. In time, we will get used to it and accept it as if it had always been so, but, for now, there is no way of making the story sound other than fantastic. It should have happened at some other time, some quiet, uneventful time, but the time was not of my choosing. Time hardly ever is.'

Then she told them about the girl in the attic who was Soobie's twin and who had slept for forty years. Only two other people knew, or were ever to know, the full story of the body in the trunk. One was Soobie, of course. The other was Joshua, for his wife had secretly told him everything because she always did. He had not really wanted to know, and he did not want to see this new daughter until she was ready to be seen.

'Does Joshua know?' asked Tulip sharply after Vinetta had finished. She herself resented deeply not being told before now.

'Yes,' said Vinetta and, for once, permitted herself a slightly insolent toss of the head.

'And when do we get to meet this granddaughter?' demanded Sir Magnus.

'Not yet,' said Vinetta firmly. 'I'll decide when, or rather Pilbeam will. I think we should all go to bed now. There has been enough excitement for one night.'

With Googles still cradled in her arms, Vinetta led the way out of the room, without a backward glance.

34. Born Knowing

'**I** WANT to talk to my granddaughter – alone.'

Sir Magnus was sitting high on his pillows. It was noon on a very dull day at the beginning of February. Pilbeam had 'come out' and been introduced to everyone individually. Vinetta, after forty years of submitting to the farce of family conferences in the big front bedroom, had at last managed to impose a little of her own reasoning on her unwieldy family.

'There will not be any ceremony. My daughter – and she is my daughter, remember – will not be forced to stand in that room and be stared at by half a dozen pairs of eyes. She will meet each one of you separately and get to know you slowly.'

Joshua said little as usual, but inwardly he applauded her decision.

Granpa was warned in advance of how it would be. He had not protested. He enjoyed the family conferences, but his store of wisdom told him that Vinetta was right.

'Pilbeam has met all of the family now, Granpa, except Appleby, of course,' said Vinetta when she finally brought the girl into his rather awesome presence.

'So I am the last to meet her,' the old man said.

'But you are the most important,' replied his daughter-in-law tactfully. 'They say you should always keep the best till last.'

Mollified, Sir Magnus looked hard at the girl standing in the doorway. Their black eyes met. Pilbeam was not in awe of him. The look was a challenge. In it there was a definite family resemblance.

It was at that moment that Sir Magnus dismissed Vinetta so that he could talk to his granddaughter alone.

'Sit there,' he said to her as Vinetta reluctantly left the room. He pointed to Tulip's armchair. Pilbeam sat down.

'What do you make of us?' he asked her. His white whiskers twitched and he waited for a shrewd answer to his shrewd question. He could remember Pilbeam now, the honest one, Soobie's twin. In the days before age and illness had confined him to his bed, he had played with her in the garden, pushing her in the swing, such a pretty child and so good-natured.

'You are my family,' said Pilbeam simply. 'What should I make of you?'

'Did they tell you that, or was it something you were born knowing?'

Pilbeam was pleased with the question. It opened the floodgates.

'Yes, Granpa, I was born knowing so many things. I know you are my family, just as I know this is my hand. I have vague memories of being a child, but I know that that must be all embedded pretend. I have sat in that attic for months, trying to figure it out. There are things I was unaccountably born knowing, things Mother and Soobie have told me, and a myriad of things that I don't know yet. I know things I shouldn't know. I am ignorant of things that should be common sense and general knowledge.'

'Do you know the town we live in?' asked Granpa. 'Do you know anything outside this house?'

'Yes,' said Pilbeam eagerly, relieved to talk to someone who was wise enough to ask the right questions. 'I know the town inside out. I know where the Market is, and Woolworths, and the Post Office. And yet it came as a surprise to me that the doors were rectangular and not all wedge-shaped like my attic door.'

'Adjustment,' murmured Granpa. 'You have slept for forty years. You are adjusting to reality. Did you dream?'

'No,' said Pilbeam, 'or if I did, I must have forgotten. I have a vague, uneasy memory of looking at Soobie's face as if it were the first thing that I had ever seen. Yet I remember the park and the lake and feeding the birds. It hurts to think about it. I am not clever enough to understand it. Though I am not sure that anybody would be.'

'Adjustment,' repeated Sir Magnus. 'Yet perhaps the best thing for you now is to forget the paradoxes. We have all lived with just such paradoxes for so long that we are totally adjusted to them.'

'Soobie's not,' interrupted Pilbeam.

'Ignore Soobie,' Granpa advised. 'Excessive introspection is no good to anyone. Know only that we are in this world, but not of it. Do you still sit in the attic?'

'Naturally,' said Pilbeam, her chin tilting defensively. 'That's where I belong.'

Magnus leant forward on his pillows and, taking his stick, thumped it hard on the floor.

'You most certainly do not belong there, young woman. You live in the house with your family. Yours is the room next to Appleby's. It always has been. I'll have no more nonsense about brooding in the attic. You'll never adjust if you stay there.'

Vinetta came in.

'Did you want something, Magnus?' she asked.

'What?' said Magnus, raising his voice.

'You banged with your stick. I thought you wanted something.'

'Take this girl to her room,' he ordered. 'And make sure she does not go back to that attic. Your own sense should tell you, it's not good for her.'

To Pilbeam he added more kindly, 'When you've got used to your room, come back here. I have some letters for you to post – and whilst you're out you can fetch me a newspaper. You might as well make yourself useful.'

Vinetta looked horrified.

'It's all right,' said Pilbeam, looking at her mother with a firmness and a confidence reminiscent of Soobie. 'I know how to do that. I'll wear the tinted spectacles and take my pink umbrella. It looks like rain.'

'The tinted spectacles?' queried Vinetta. 'Your pink umbrella?'

'Yes,' said Pilbeam, 'they're in my room.'

'Your room?' echoed Vinetta again.

'The room next to Appleby's. It is mine. It has always been mine.'

Vinetta too needed to adjust.

'Of course,' she said. 'What am I thinking of?'

In a surprisingly short time, Pilbeam became part of the family as if she had always been there. Some members tactfully pretended she had never been asleep in the attic, others, better skilled in pretence, totally forgot. In their corporate adjustment, the graceful girl with the jet-black hair and smouldering eyes developed as complete a past as any of them. They all did their share, threading Pilbeam into the family history until she became part of the fabric.

It was a very complex procedure, because, like them, she could remember being the child she had never been; but unlike them, her memory also had to invent experiences for the past real forty years. They all co-operated.

'Do you remember when Dad was Santa Claus?' asked Wimpey one day.

'Yes,' said Pilbeam truthfully, 'and Appleby took you both to see him. I told her not to, but she wouldn't listen to me.'

And Wimpey remembered well the argument and Pilbeam's exasperation. The long sleep in the attic had never happened. Pilbeam had always been with them.

35. Appleby's Progress

PILBEAM had not been allowed to see Appleby. The airing-cupboard door was kept shut.

'You understand, don't you, Pilbeam?' Vinetta said. 'It wouldn't be fair to let you see her as she is now. In a little while she should be ready to meet you.'

'Does she know about me?' demanded Pilbeam.

Vinetta sighed. Life was so complicated now. She had never reckoned on life being complicated. It was like knitting on a dozen different needles.

'I really don't know,' she answered. 'I have tried telling her, but I don't know how much she has heard. She seems to be in some sort of coma. I look in two or three times a day and I talk to her a little but there is never a response. Her arms still ooze a little water when I squeeze them. We've changed the bath-towels under her chair every week. They are drier now than they were at first, of course, but there is still a dampness about them.'

'I wish I could help,' said Pilbeam.

'Your turn will come,' said Vinetta wisely. 'When she is better she will be glad of a friend. It could be the making of her. Aunt Kate always intended the two of you to be friends. Memories of things I was born knowing are expanding to include your friendship.'

'I know,' said Pilbeam emphatically. 'The same is happening to me. It will be so much easier when she is well again; things will slot into place better. I hate pretending. I wish the pretend bit were safely over.'

In the months she had spent in the airing cupboard, Appleby had never spoken. The little brass bell on the floor beside her chair had never been rung. She made no attempt at all to communicate with anybody. Vinetta worried and worried, but the worrying achieved nothing.

Then one day, towards the end of March, there was a glimmer of hope. The towels on the floor were, for the first time, bone dry.

It was mid-morning. Everybody else in the house was about their business. Vinetta always made sure of that. The airing-cupboard door was open and the light from the landing window shone in. Appleby, looking immaculately clean and, outwardly at least, absolutely dry, turned her head and looked at her mother. It was so unexpected that Vinetta was taken by surprise.

'You are looking at me!' she exclaimed. 'You are really looking at me!'

Appleby's look became fixed and Vinetta's hopes felt crushed. The head had definitely turned, the eyes had flickered intelligently. But now it was gone again.

Just as Vinetta was closing the door, a strangely cracked little voice said, 'I think I'll go to my own room now.'

Vinetta was careful not to show any surprise this time. She opened the door wide again and grasped Appleby's right arm.

'Let me help you,' she said in a voice that combined comfort with matter-of-factness. Without another word, she took her daughter to her bedroom and settled her down on her own bed.

'I'll bring your chair back now,' she said, trying to return everything to normal.

'No,' said Appleby looking petulant. 'I never want to see that chair again. You can buy me a new one.'

'I'll buy you anything you want,' promised her mother rashly. 'I must go and tell the others you are better. We have all been so worried about you.'

'Don't let them come here,' snapped Appleby. 'I don't want to see any of them yet. And I don't want to see you either. Go away. And stay away.'

It was the old Appleby, no mistaking it! After all she had done, anyone else would have been subdued at least, ashamed, apologetic, pleasant. Not Appleby Mennym. She was as defiant and unpleasant and as independent as ever.

Vinetta left the room without another word, but she came back a few seconds later with Tulip's brass bell in her hand. She put it down on the table beside Appleby's bed.

'If you want anything,' she said, 'just ring.'

She longed to hug her daughter and rejoice that she was on the mend, but the green eyes glowered and warned her to keep her distance. Vinetta looked like a faithful spaniel, happy but deeply hurt. On due reflection the hurt might turn to anger, but this bitter-sweet sorrow was uppermost for now.

'All right, all right,' said Appleby, looking uncomfortably at her mother's sad face. 'Now you can go away and leave me alone.'

Christmas had come and gone in the time Appleby spent in the airing cupboard. A bleak Christmas it had been too, with no presents and no celebrations. Soobie, with no word to anyone, had gone to the church and managed to light a candle. That was all. Easter came and went whilst Appleby stayed in her room, and the brass bell never rang.

'Don't look in on her,' advised Sir Magnus when Vinetta told him of Appleby's hardness. 'You'll only provoke her more. When she is ready, she will come out. She will come out more quickly if she thinks no one is taking any notice of her.'

'But she's been ill, Magnus,' protested Vinetta. 'She's been very ill. Not one of us has ever been so ill before.'

'She's not ill now,' said her grandfather. 'If she is being cheeky to you, she's well on the way back to health. All you have to do now is wait.'

'I could take her some pretend beef tea,' suggested Vinetta. 'She has always liked pretends.'

'No,' insisted Sir Magnus. 'Wait. Do nothing. Be patient.'

'Waiting is not easy,' said Vinetta.

'It won't be easy for her either,' said Magnus shrewdly. 'Now you'll have to leave me. I have work to do. My publisher is not waiting for an article on the life and times of Appleby Mennym.'

36. More Letters

SIR MAGNUS was the first to think of it. One afternoon, at the beginning of April, he called Tulip to his bedside.

'Take this,' he said 'and push it under Appleby's door. Don't go in. Don't even knock.'

It was a small brown envelope with 'Miss Appleby Mennym' written in neat script on the back.

Tulip raised her eyebrows but said nothing. As she passed Appleby's room she slid the letter under the door. With her usual quickness, she went straight on and about her own business. Vinetta, no doubt, would have waited and listened for sounds from inside the room, but not Tulip.

Appleby, lying on her bed and getting more and more bored by the minute, saw the envelope edge its way through the door. She waited at least half an hour before going to pick it up. She wouldn't give them the satisfaction of hearing her move, if that was what they were waiting for. She did not trust any of them.

'My dearest Grand-daughter,' she read, when at last she decided to retrieve it and open it, 'We have had enough of this stuff and nonsense. It is making your mother very upset. Pull yourself together, girl, and come and join the family. There'll be no reference to things past, no recriminations. No one will ever mention the name of Albert Pond.
Your loving Granpa,
Magnus Mennym'

'Some hopes!' exclaimed Appleby. 'The minute I'm out of that door it'll be "Why ever did you do it?", "Where did you go?", "How did you get so dirty?" and those twins might even ask if it was fun.'

Taking the airmail stationery, of which she still had a fairly large supply, she tore off a flimsy blue sheet and wrote in large letters the words:

GET STUFFED

Then she put it in an airmail envelope and addressed it in her best handwriting to 'Sir Magnus Mennym'.

It was Vinetta who picked up the envelope as she was on her way to Granpa's room in the early evening, just after the family hour.

Sir Magnus took his silver paperknife and opened it with a flourish. When he read the contents he nearly bounced out of his bed with rage.

'There'll have to be a conference,' he shouted. 'Tell everybody to come here now, this minute. Even Miss Quigley.'

Vinetta glimpsed the words on the paper as it fluttered to the floor. Then she steeled herself to say what she had to say.

'There will be no conferences. There have been too many already. Leave it be. I'll write to her. She's obviously willing to read letters and to answer them, however objectionable the answers may be.'

Sir Magnus still looked furious. 'A conference . . .' he spluttered, black beady eyes popping.

'Stop that,' said Vinetta sharply. 'If you don't you might just be the first rag doll ever to die of a stroke. Leave it to me. I know what I am doing.'

The next letter Appleby received was from her mother.

'Dear Appleby,' she read, 'I won't dwell on anything wrong you may have done. I can't be your judge. I can't even be so condescending as to forgive you. How do I know what there is to forgive?

All I can offer you is my unconditional love. And if you come out, there will be nothing said to you about the past, not by me, not by anyone. No doubt Granpa made you a similar promise. There is a difference. I will make sure, absolutely sure, that the promise is kept. I have never realised till now just how much power I have in this family. I can restrain them and I will.

If some day you wanted to talk to me about what happened, I would be happy to listen. But you would have to speak first. I will never broach the subject with you again. The truth is a gift in your possession. You can decide to keep it, or to bestow it on whomever you choose. No one will ever ask you any questions. We can pretend it never happened, if that is what you want.

Please join us. We love you. Do not make yourself a stranger.

Mother'

*

Appleby sobbed when she read the letter. She read it two or three times and then put it away safely in a drawer.

Taking paper again, she wrote on it just two words:

I CAN'T

Pilbeam it was who found the airmail envelope addressed to Vinetta. She dashed down with it to the kitchen where Vinetta was busy ironing.

'She still won't come out,' sighed Vinetta.

Pilbeam, looking over her mother's shoulder, corrected her.

'She doesn't say "won't". She says "can't".'

'It amounts to the same thing.'

'No, it doesn't. She says "can't" and I think she really means it. I almost understand her. She is my sister, after all, and nearer my age than any of yours.'

'You don't even know her,' said Vinetta bitterly.

'Yes, I do,' declared Pilbeam with sudden clarity of vision. 'I was born knowing her.'

At those words, with that thought, the next move became obvious.

'I am going up to see her,' she said.

'Don't,' said Vinetta anxiously, but Pilbeam was already out of the kitchen door and halfway up the first flight of stairs. Vinetta hurried after her. They paused outside Appleby's door. Pilbeam knocked once, quite firmly. There was no reply. So she pushed open the door.

'Who are you?' screamed Appleby. 'Get out of here. This is my room.'

'I'm Pilbeam,' answered Pilbeam sharply. 'I'm your sister and Soobie's twin. You know perfectly well who I am. So stop being stupid.'

Pilbeam went into the room. Vinetta, standing in the hall, had the good sense not to follow. She closed the door and, a little reluctantly, left them to sort it out between themselves.

The next day, Appleby rejoined the family. She became her old, perky, abrasive self again. There were no apologies, not even an explanation. Nobody mentioned Albert Pond. For good or ill, that was what Vinetta decreed and everyone was made to agree to it. It was her side of the bargain. Like the old lease on the house, it was very much in favour of the owner. In this case, the owner was Appleby; the property, her mother's unconditional love.

37. Miss Quigley's Champions

'MISS QUIGLEY never comes to visit now,' said Pilbeam, who was still adjusting to knowing things she had been told and to recognising things that, being part of her fictional sixteen years' experience of life, she was born knowing.

She and Appleby were sitting in the lounge on a coldish day in May. They had established their own cosy corner, well away from Soobie's bay window, well away from the fireplace where the grown-ups had their own special seats. In the corner where they sat they had placed the round table with the claw feet, brought down from the attic, and two comfortable, cushioned basket armchairs with very high, wide-curved backs, bought for them by Vinetta from a catalogue. A long, narrow side window gave them a view of the front path.

'You're right, you know,' agreed Appleby. 'I haven't seen her since – well, for ages. She used to come at least once a fortnight.'

In fact, Miss Quigley had not come out of her cupboard since Granpa Mennym's last conference. She had said she never came if she wasn't invited and the perverse woman, always a stickler for what she thought of as protocol, was determined to wait for an invitation, however long it might be in coming. 'I could be dead for all they know,' she said to herself as the weeks went by, '– or care, for that matter.'

'She could be dead,' said Pilbeam, not quite knowing what being dead meant. It happened in books. Aunt Kate had died, but no one really remembered that.

'Let's ask Mother about her,' suggested Appleby. 'After all, she's *her* friend.'

Vinetta was in the kitchen, pretending to bake a cake.

'What is it?' she asked, pausing in mid-stir with the wooden spoon in her hand and the earthenware bowl cradled under her arm.

'We were wondering about Miss Quigley,' began Pilbeam.

'Goodness!' cried Vinetta, as startled as if she had left something burning in the oven. 'I'd forgotten all about her. She hasn't been round for ages. I'll write her a proper invitation to tea. She'll like that.'

'No,' said Pilbeam, who could be as forthright as her twin on occasions. 'You know perfectly well that she's sitting in the hall cupboard and is probably as miserable as can be. What right have we to forget her? It's disgraceful. She should have a room in the house. She was made here, same as we were.'

'There isn't a room,' said Vinetta wildly. She put the basin down on the kitchen table and let the wooden spoon clatter into it.

'There is,' said Appleby, ready to back up her sister. 'There's the guest room under Pilbeam's.'

'That's the guest room,' protested Vinetta. 'It is meant for occasional visitors.'

'We never have occasional visitors. I've never heard such rubbish.' Pilbeam raised her voice and looked really angry.

Vinetta faced the two united teenagers whose gaze was one of determined accusation. Sometimes nothing but the truth will do. Vinetta wrung her hands and spoke.

'They don't like her. Granpa Mennym can't stand her. He feels guilty about it and always insists upon her being told things, but she gets on his nerves. Tulip says she can only take her in small doses. The twins are terrified to make a noise when she's here. And your father never speaks two words to her.'

'Dad never speaks two words to anybody,' said Pilbeam scornfully, remembering how he had looked at her when they had first met.

'All right then?' he had asked awkwardly.

'Yes,' said Pilbeam, for what else could she say?

'All right then,' Joshua had concluded before sitting in the armchair to read the newspaper and suck his unlit pipe. Pilbeam had not minded his gruffness. It was a comfortable, tacit acceptance of her being there. But she still felt free to poke fun at it.

'And as for the others,' chipped in Appleby, 'they're no better than she is. We are no better. We all get on each other's nerves from time to time.'

It was a very mature thought coming from Appleby, but Vinetta chose to ignore it.

'She cannot live in the house,' she insisted. 'She is not, and has never been, one of the family.'

'That's terrible,' Pilbeam exploded. 'You're horrible. And I don't care if you are my mother. You would see that poor woman cooped up forever in a cupboard and just be nice to her when you choose to. I can't believe it.'

It was extremely difficult for Vinetta to re-adjust. This was how it had been for forty years. Miss Quigley had never objected. Once she had stayed the weekend in the guest room they now proposed should be her permanent home. It had been a pleasant pretend at first, but then the visitor had irritated everyone by saying too much and getting in the way, then apologising profusely before getting in the way again.

'When is she going back to Trevicky Street?' Wimpey had asked in a stage whisper.

Miss Quigley had heard, as she was meant to, but she had said nothing. Within the hour she had appeared in the hall, carrying her tartan weekend bag.

'I'll have to be getting home now,' she had said to Vinetta. 'I have so many things to do. But it has been a lovely weekend. I've enjoyed every minute of it. Still, one mustn't overstay one's welcome.'

'Nonsense,' said Vinetta as she held open the front door. 'You know we love to have you, Hortensia. You must come again when you have the time.'

'I'll see,' Miss Quigley had said a bit bleakly. 'It's hard to get away, you know. I can't always be asking the neighbours to look after the plants and the cat.'

That was all of fifteen years ago. She had never stayed again.

'Miss Quigley wouldn't agree to stay here anyway,' said Vinetta, on firmer ground. 'She's too proud to take charity.'

'She would come if she felt she was useful,' said Pilbeam astutely.

'And you tell me how she could be useful,' said Vinetta grimly.

'She could look after Googles for you. She could be a sort of nanny,' suggested Pilbeam.

'I don't need a nanny. I look after Googles myself.'

'When you remember,' said Appleby sarcastically. 'You're always too busy being a housewife or sitting at your sewing machine. You're never any fun. Googles just lies there all day and you don't even talk to her. You just go through the ritual of giving her a bottle and changing her nappy and then you plonk her down again like a bag of carrots.'

Vinetta was furious.

'She's a very good baby anyway. She doesn't take a lot of looking after. And I must say I've never noticed you paying any attention to her.'

'Why should I pay any attention to her? She's not mine. I've got more to do with my time. I'm telling you – you should offer the job to Miss Quigley.'

'I agree,' said Pilbeam. 'It's the best possible solution. Googles would like it. She might even learn to talk.'

Vinetta looked guilty.

'She's not meant to talk. She's only six months old.'

'She could get to be nine months old. She doesn't have to stand absolutely still. I'm sometimes fourteen and sometimes fifteen,' put in Appleby with unusual honesty.

The chink in Vinetta's armour was that she had always thought herself the perfect mother – protective, efficient and, above all, fair and reasonable. It was embarrassing to face up to the fact that she was not perfect for Googles, but the fair and reasonable side of her character forced her to listen to their arguments. She gave in and set herself to the usual business of reconciling the rest of the household to the inevitable. They were all surprisingly gracious when it came to the point.

'I have often thought she shouldn't be living where she lives,' said Granny Tulip without specifying whether she meant Trevethick Street or the cupboard, 'and you have always been fond of her, Vinetta. She's just like one of the family.'

'If she lived here,' reasoned Poopie, 'we wouldn't have to be quiet all the time. She wouldn't be a visitor, would she?'

'I like her anyway,' said Wimpey. 'I never said I didn't, did I?'

Soobie satisfied himself with saying bluntly, 'It's about time. Pretending that cupboard is Trevethick Street is the daftest pretend I've ever had to put up with.'

Granpa Mennym had some reservations, but he expressed them tactfully. 'I think she's a bit afraid of me, but she needn't come into my room at all. Conferences are few and far between now.'

Joshua's was the one openly dissenting voice.

'She's too fussy, Vinetta. And she talks too much.'

Joshua was the only one in the family who would not have minded spending weeks in the hall cupboard, so it was harder to make him feel guilty.

'She won't need to talk so much,' argued Vinetta, 'if she doesn't spend so much time on her own. And she's coming anyway. So you might as well get used to the idea.'

38. Miss Quigley Settles In

MISS QUIGLEY took over Soobie's room. 'You are sure you don't mind, dear?' Vinetta had asked anxiously.

'Of course I don't mind. I offered, didn't I? It was obvious we couldn't put her on the same landing as the twins. There'd have been ructions. And you couldn't ask Appleby or Pilbeam to move downstairs. I'm the only one you could move.'

'But you've always had that room,' persisted Vinetta.

'Mother, Mother, you are beginning to sound like Miss Quigley yourself. A room is just a room. I honestly don't care which room I have. Besides, it's one less flight of stairs,' he joked.

Miss Quigley was grateful, but, surprisingly, not overgrateful. If they had expected her to gush and flutter, they would have been disappointed.

'I won't be a visitor here anymore,' she had said with satisfaction. 'If I wish to return to Trevethick Street, it will be for a short vacation. I will be entitled to holidays, you know. All employees are.'

Vinetta was surprised at her businesslike way of dealing with her new situation. She and Tulip agreed on a reasonable live-in wage, to be paid into Miss Quigley's own bank account every month.

'And I shall need time off for myself,' she added, 'in which I can follow my own pursuits and recreations.'

When Sir Magnus was told about how the worm had turned, he said simply, 'Good for her. About time she stuck up for herself.'

When she first took up her post, at the beginning of June, Appleby and Pilbeam put a vase full of roses in her room.

'They're beautiful,' she said. 'Thank you very much for being so thoughtful. But you must remember I am not a guest anymore. I am an employee of your mother's.'

The girls looked disappointed. She was their protégée. They had been responsible for bringing her into the house and they had assumed that they would go on protecting her interests and generally looking after her.

Miss Quigley saw the disappointment in their faces and gave them the smile a grown-up gives to children.

'I'm delighted at the welcome you have given me,' she said. 'You are both very good girls. Your mother must be proud of you.'

'Can we help you to . . .'

Whatever help Appleby was going to offer, she was cut short.

'I don't need any help, my dears. Though it's kind of you to offer.'

To Vinetta, she was still Hortensia, and her new employer insisted upon Miss Quigley calling her Vinetta, as she had always done.

'Wouldn't "ma'am" be more appropriate?' Hortensia had asked doubtfully.

'No, it would not, Hortensia. We aren't living in the nineteenth century. You do a job. I pay you for it. But outside of that, we are still friends.'

And they were. They were better friends than ever, sitting together and chatting and making all sorts of plans.

On her days off, Miss Quigley went out. It soon became apparent that she was as keen on going out as Appleby had ever been. Not only that, she was brilliant at passing by unnoticed. Nobody pays much attention to a dowdy, frumpish, middle-aged woman, but, over and above that, Hortensia Quigley had some strange power of deflecting attention from her person. Nobody ever really saw her, because she made sure that nobody ever looked.

She went shopping. She joined the public library. And one day she brought home some very large rectangular packages.

'They look interesting,' Vinetta had said when she met her at the door and helped her in with them. Yet that was all she ventured to say. The new Miss Quigley brooked no intrusion. She had lived too long in the hall cupboard to feel any need to confide in anyone, or to permit anyone to question her.

'They're my art things,' she said briefly. 'I'll be able to paint again.'

And, naturally, Vinetta said no more.

Even when she set up her easel in the back garden one warm, sunny afternoon, it was some time before anyone approached to look at what she was doing. She sat there on her folding stool in her voile flowered dress and pale green cardigan, her thin brown hair tied back neatly into an absurdly small bun. The sun shone down on her hunched shoulders and her grey-mittened hands as she deftly held her palette and changed from one brush to another in a very expert-looking way.

She was painting a picture of the sky. Low down in the foreground it was staring blankly through the leafy branches of a tree. But the sky that stretched far, far up above the tree, dwarfing it, was full of emotion, gleams of hopeful light and shadows like frowning faces. It was a curious picture, top-heavy and vaguely oppressive.

When Pilbeam ventured to look over her shoulder at last, she said, 'It's lovely, Miss Quigley, but a bit frightening. You have made the sky look so much more . . .' she looked for the right word – 'important than the tree.'

'The sky is more important than the tree. Quite clever of you to notice, Pilbeam. I'm what you might call a symbolist painter. A little symbolism never comes in wrong, does it?' Hortensia Quigley's plain face was brightened by something that came as near to a grin as a lady of her age and temperament could produce. Pilbeam did not quite understand, was slightly startled by the grin, and said no more.

No one ever asked Miss Quigley how she had learned to paint. In their household it was an unnecessary question. It was obviously something she had been born knowing.

As nurse to Googles, she showed another side to her nature. Routine was important, as one would expect even of the old Miss Quigley, but no one could have expected her to concern herself so much with the baby's happiness. She took her to the park. Vinetta had never dared to do that because she was afraid strangers might look into the pram. No such fears beset Miss Quigley, She bought the baby interesting toys, prisms and mobiles, tops that hummed and clocks that ticked and sang. Googles became more real. True, she cried more, but she laughed more too, a hearty, chortly laugh that made you want to join in.

'I don't know how we ever managed without Hortensia,' Vinetta said to Joshua as they sat in the lounge early one evening. Hortensia and the baby only ever appeared for five minutes, just before Joshua went out to work, so that Googles could say, 'Dada ... Dada' and wave him goodbye.

'She's good with the baby,' agreed Joshua. 'I'll grant you that.' It was reluctant approval. Joshua, you remember, had opposed bringing that silly woman into the house, but even he had to admit it had turned out better than expected.

Tulip soon became reconciled to having Miss Quigley on the pay-roll, as it were. She did a very good job. If the grandmother felt a twinge of jealousy that a stranger should so obviously have captured the baby's heart, she knew to suppress such an unworthy thought.

Poopie and Wimpey ignored Miss Quigley's existence, and she ignored theirs. She was not being paid to look after them. They were not part of her duties and she had no intention of being exploited.

She never saw Sir Magnus, even though her room was on the same landing. What the old man heard of her these days, he liked. But he was still happy enough not to see her. She couldn't have changed that much, was his thought. He was content to admire her new achievements from afar. Her *Clouds before a Storm* hung over his mantelpiece, paid for by cheque and a neat note expressing approval and appreciation.

39. The Last Chapter

'I MADE up Albert Pond. Did they tell you?' Appleby nodded towards the house.

She and Pilbeam were sitting on the white bench in the back garden on an idyllic afternoon. It was June again and warm and sunny. The lawn had just been trimmed that morning by Poopie. The flower borders were blooming with pansies, sweet peas and a profusion of other soft, small-petalled flowers, all whites and pale pinks and blues. The only other person out there was Miss Quigley, and she was seated in a spot well away from the girls.

Appleby's remark was made quite out of the blue. Albert Pond's name had not been mentioned for more than a year.

'Of course they told me,' replied Pilbeam with just the merest toss of the head. 'They tell me everything. They still think I have such a lot of catching up to do.'

Appleby thought for a moment that Pilbeam was going to be cross with her again. Pilbeam was such a stickler for getting the record straight, and she wouldn't put up with any nonsense.

'I didn't mean to do it, really,' she went on hastily. 'At least, I didn't mean it to snowball the way it did. But once I'd started and they all believed it, I didn't know how to stop. I even began to believe in him myself. If Chesney Loftus hadn't died, I probably would have got away with it.'

Pilbeam considered this. She herself would never have been in that predicament. She would never have thought of inventing Albert Pond. It was as much as she could do to pretend to be eating Sunday lunch. She would sit across the table from Soobie and exchange sympathetic glances as they dutifully held knives and forks above empty plates.

'I'll never understand you properly,' she said, 'but they should. Except for me and Soobie, they all have their own pretends of one sort or another.'

Appleby shrugged but said nothing.

'Where did you get the name from?' asked Pilbeam. 'Albert Pond is not what I would call charismatic.'

'Well, I like it,' Appleby bristled. 'I have always liked it. As a matter of fact, it is a real name. It was written ten times over inside the front cover of a book I found years ago in the cupboard under the windowseat in my room. I've still got the book. It's called *Greenmantle*. I reckon Albert Pond was bored silly some day and decided to doodle on it. His name list ends with three anagrams: Bold Parent, Planet Drob and Bored Plant.'

Pilbeam looked intrigued and Appleby, who was beginning to feel a bit uncomfortable under questioning, tried to play the advantage.

'I had a go with my name,' she went on, 'but all I could manage was "Be my penny lamp". Not enough vowels, you see. Yours might be better.'

But Pilbeam was not so easily distracted.

'What about the letters?' she persisted. 'Why Australia? And how did you manage the postmarks?'

'Easy,' answered Appleby triumphantly. This was not the question she feared. 'I had some foreign covers I bought from a catalogue. And I had loads of used stamps to choose from. The covers had airmail stickers on them. At first, I just wondered if I could fake up a cover with our address on it. I used inkpad ink to continue the postmark off the stamp on to the envelope. Then I steamed a sticker off one of my Australian covers and gummed it on. When I'd finished it looked so convincing I couldn't resist the temptation to use it.'

Pilbeam gave this some thought. She could see how one thing had led to another.

'And when it all came out, you ran away. What good did you think running away would do?'

Appleby looked frightened.

'You're not supposed to ask me anything about that. Mother said nobody was to mention it.'

Pilbeam got up from the bench angrily.

'You started talking about Albert Pond, not me. You want to make your mind up. But I'll tell you this, Appleby Mennym, if there are things I can't ask you, I am not going to be your friend. I can't help being your sister, but there's nothing says I have to be friends with you.'

That was a terrible threat. By now it seemed as if they had been friends for years and years, going out together arm in arm, giggling and joking, reading the same magazines, following the same fashions, lazing in the garden when the sun shone down. To quarrel with Pilbeam would be dreadful, and she might mean what she said, they might never be friends again. The thought was unbearable.

Appleby reached up and tugged Pilbeam by the arm before she could stomp off.

'Please sit down again. I'm sorry. I'll tell you anything you want to know, but you must promise faithfully never to tell them.'

Again Appleby nodded towards the house. Inside, the reals and the pretends were all in progress – real accounts, pretend invitations which would have to be reluctantly refused, real ironing, pretend cakes being mixed quite vigorously in the earthenware bowl, real rest and the pretend smoking of a beloved pipe and a long, Havana cigar, real toys and pretend games of cowboys and Indians.

'They tell me everything,' repeated Pilbeam as she sat down again, 'but I tell them nothing unless it suits me. And I wouldn't dream of telling them anything you didn't want them to know. And we are friends, now and for always.'

Appleby started a bit incoherently, but Pilbeam understood.

'They would have gone on and on at me, about all the expense I'd put them to for darker curtains and low-watt light bulbs, and they would have made a meal of how terrified Miss Quigley had been, as if they cared two hoots about Miss Quigley. I couldn't stand it. They'd have expected me to say sorry. I never say sorry.'

'You say sorry to me,' said Pilbeam.

'You're different. You're my friend. And you never try to make me say sorry, like telling me to sit up and beg. When I say sorry to you, it's because I want to say sorry.'

'And because you know you are in the wrong,' insisted Pilbeam, anxious as always to stick to the absolute truth.

'I know I am in the wrong with them too,' admitted Appleby. 'That makes it harder if anything. I know what I did was terrible, but I wouldn't tell them that. I wouldn't give them the satisfaction.'

'Running away was worse than all the lies,' put in Pilbeam, determined to get Appleby back to her original question.

'I know,' sighed Appleby. 'It was a nightmare. I remember standing in Granpa's room with them all looking at me, wondering what was coming next, and I just ran out.'

'What did you mean to do?'

'I don't know. Probably sneak back later, the way Miss Quigley used to. But then I got further and further away from the house. The rain was lashing down. I went into the park and hid in a shelter.'

The memory of that night made Appleby shudder.

'You needn't tell me any more if you don't want to,' said Pilbeam gently.

'I do,' said Appleby. "I suppose that's why I mentioned Albert Pond to you in the first place. A bit of me wants to forget all about it, but another bit needs to talk. It was so terrible, Pilbeam, you can't imagine how terrible. Three skinheads in studded leather jackets came into the shelter. They were livid when they saw me sitting there. They had obviously been up to no good. They swore at me and I ran out into the dark. I was terrified and I couldn't see where I was going. I kept my head down against the rain and the next thing I knew I'd tripped over a little iron railing into the lake. I crawled out, wet through. I couldn't move properly. I wriggled into some bushes and I must have gone to sleep. I knew vaguely that day came and the church bells were ringing. Then night came again and then another day. And, do you know, Pilbeam, there comes a time when if you are not going to die, you begin to make some attempt to get back to living.

'I crawled out of the bushes as soon as the park closed and made my way towards the lights on the path. I skirted the green and got up to the old shop where they used to sell pop and sweets in summer, before they built the new place. By then I was exhausted again. So I lay on a seat to rest, and that is where Soobie found me.'

Pilbeam was silent.

Appleby waited for her to speak, but when the silence became uncomfortable she added aggressively, 'So now you know. I hope you're satisfied.'

Pilbeam put one arm round Appleby's shoulders in a hug.

'I was just thinking,' she said. 'If you hadn't told all those lies in the first place, I wouldn't be here. I would still be asleep in the trunk in the attic. I could have been left there for another forty years.'

At this thought, Appleby brightened.

'And if I hadn't run away,' she reasoned, 'Miss Quigley would still be living a half-life in the cupboard in the hall. It was only my time in the airing cupboard that made me realise how awful her life must have been.'

At the other end of the garden, sheltered by the yew hedge, Miss Quigley was seated at her easel painting a lone, white cloud that drifted slowly along, very high up, in the silky blue sky. In the carrycot by her side, Googles was lying kicking her feet and rattling a pink plastic bear with considerable enthusiasm.

As Appleby watched them, a little humility crept in. She looked shyly at her sister.

'And I needed you, Nuova Pilbeam,' she said softly. 'You'll never know how much I needed you.'

Extra!

Extra!

READ ALL ABOUT IT!

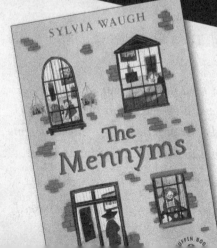

SYLVIA WAUGH

The
Mennyms

SYLVIA WAUGH

1935	Born in Gateshead in the north-east of England
1959–62	Teaches at the Bede Grammar School for Girls in Sunderland. From the mid-1960s to early 1970s works as a part-time teacher, and has three children
1976–87	Resumes full-time teaching at a high school within easy travelling distance of home
1987	Takes early retirement and is able to devote more time to her writing
1993	Her first novel, The Mennyms, is published and is an immediate success
1994	The Mennyms wins the Guardian Children's Fiction Prize, and is shortlisted for the prestigious Carnegie Medal. Continues to write the Mennyms series. Mennyms in the Wilderness is published
1995	Mennyms Under Siege is published
1996	Mennyms Alone, and Mennyms Alive, are published

1997	*Sylvia wins the highly prestigious Dutch Zilveren Zoen (The Silver Kiss) Award for* The Mennyms
1999	*In July her first grandson is born. Sylvia becomes his childminder and continues to write*
2000	*The Mennyms series wins the Austrian Kinderbuchpreis in Vienna.* Space Race, *the first title in The Ormingat Trilogy, is published*
2002	Earthborn, *the second book in The Ormingat Trilogy is published*
2003	*In August Sylvia's second grandson is born.* Who Goes Home?, *the final instalment in The Ormingat Trilogy is published.*
2004–present day	*Sylvia continues to write every day on a variety of topics and is still very engaged with all her published books, including ideas for the* Mennyms *as film, musical and stage productions.*

INTERESTING FACTS

Sylvia Waugh was born not long before the beginning of the Second World War. She has lived most of her life in the north-east of England. Her earliest happy memories include frequent visits to Saltwell Park in Gateshead, to run on the green, feed the ducks and play on the swings. And, less frequently, trips down to Newcastle Quayside Market on a Sunday morning. Her favourite bridge is the little Swing Bridge, built around the time her great-grandmother was born.

In 2015 a set of hand-made life-size Mennym dolls appeared at the Isle of Wight Festival! Created by the Ryde Mennyms, a project group set up to celebrate Sylvia's award-winning series, the Ryde Mennyms then went on tour to Roehampton University in London and to Gateshead Library in Tyne-and-Wear where they were visited by many children from local schools.

Sylvia's original manuscripts are archived at Seven Stories National Centre for Children's Books in Newcastle-upon-Tyne – a museum, library and visitors' centre set up to preserve the wonderful British heritage of writing and illustrations for children.

Sylvia is a natural and contented homemaker with a family of three grown-up children and two very nearly grown-up grandchildren.

The Mennyms stories are read and loved all over the world, from America to Australia to Japan, with much of Europe in between, and they have won many international prizes and commendations. It amazed her when so many people, children and grown-ups, other writers as well as readers, loved the Mennyms and wrote to her about them. And it still happens today.

The Ormingat Trilogy are stories about civilized, unscary aliens from far away in outer space who live among us but do not present any threat to the world. The world becomes a threat to them.

WHERE DID THE
STORY COME FROM?

*Sylvia describes herself as a 'contrary' writer – she
doesn't write in order to please readers but writes in
the hope that they will be pleased with what she has
written. Although she is aware of the many stories
drawn from life in the big wide world, Sylvia says that
she has very little experience outside of her own world
where crime and poverty have no place at all, and neither
does wealth and big-spending. The world she knows is
one of 'ordinary' people and places, but in truth, she says,
no one is really ordinary. We are all individuals, making
our way in the world, taking the opportunities that come
along. Sylvia says, 'In the Mennyms books there is no
wickedness, just a deep desire to live useful and interesting
and private lives. They don't always score and things do
go wrong – but the intention to hurt is not there. So my
readers are invited into my books to meet people like
themselves who just happen to be rag dolls.'*

GUESS WHO?

A — He had been born knowing a thousand pearls of wisdom.

B — 'We may be strange. I know we are strange. But surely we are not horrific?'

C — Her limbs and torso, full of water, looked bloated. Her cheeks were abnormally plump so that the green button eyes were almost lost in their folds.

D — 'I'm just past thirty, unmarried (and with no intentions in that direction) and I must've spent more time with sheep than with people for the past ten years or more.'

E — 'It is just I find it hard to accept being a rag doll in a world that is obviously designed for human beings.'

WORDS GLORIOUS WORDS!

We often come across **new** or **unfamiliar** words when we're reading. Here are a few unusual words you'll find in this Puffin book. Did you spot any others?

hale   *strong and healthy, used when referring to an elderly person*

surreptitiously   *in a way that attempts to avoid notice or attention*

jamboree   *a large, merry social gathering of people*

hoity-toity   *assuming airs, pretentious or haughty*

bobby-soxer   *an adolescent girl, especially during the 1940s, following youthful fads and fashions*

flounce   *to go about with impatient, impetuous or exaggerated movements*

irascible   *having or showing a tendency to be easily angered*

myriad   *a countless or extremely great number of people or things*

QUIZ

1
Where in the world does Albert Pond reside?

a) *China*

b) *Egypt*

c) *Australia*

d) *Brazil*

2
What football team does Joshua support?

a) *Aston Villa*

b) *Port Vale*

c) *Accrington Stanley*

d) *Tottenham Hotspurs*

3 *Who takes care of the house accounts?*

a) *Tulip*

b) *Soobie*

c) *Sir Magnus*

d) *Appleby*

4 *How long had Pilbeam been asleep in the attic?*

a) *One hundred years*

b) *Two weeks*

c) *She was actually asleep in the basement*

d) *Forty years*

5 *Who eventually finds Appleby in the park?*

a) *Pilbeam*

b) *Soobie*

c) *The police*

d) *Sir Magnus*

IN THIS YEAR

1993 Fact Pack

What else was happening in the world when this Puffin book was published?

Buckingham Palace opens its doors to the public for the first time.

Steven Spielberg's **Jurassic Park** *is the highest-grossing film of the year.*

A tsunami reaching over 10m high hits the coast of Hokkaido, Japan, in July.

MAKE AND DO

Create your own member of the Mennym family!

There is always room for one more at 5 Brocklehurst Grove! Make up your own Mennym character to join Appleby, Soobie and the gang.

YOU WILL NEED:

* Plain card
* Colouring pencils or felt-tips
* A pencil
* Glue
* Spare fabric
* Buttons
* Scissors

Draw an outline of your Mennym on a piece of card. They could be long and lean like Appleby or a small tot like Googles.

 Find some spare bits of fabric from around the house.

 With a pencil trace the outline of an outfit for your Mennym on the pieces of fabric. Carefully cut these out and stick them on to your Mennym's body.

4 Using your coloured pencils decorate the rest of your Mennym. Will they be blue like Soobie, stylish like Appleby or prim and proper like Tulip?

 Carefully cut out the outline of the body.

6 Find two buttons for eyes and glue them on to your Mennym to bring them to life!

7 Think about the backstory of your new Mennym and give them an appropriate name. How are they related to the family and what are their personality traits? Write about their adventures and how they avoid being discovered by human beings!

DID YOU KNOW?

Rag dolls are amongst the oldest toys in existence. The British Museum is home to a Roman rag doll dating back from between the 1st–5th century AD.

Original rag dolls often had no facial features!

Rag dolls are an economical alternative to shop-bought toys. They can be stitched together from pieces of spare material – anything from old socks to unwanted tea cloths!

Rag dolls have featured in many popular children's stories and TV shows over the years. As well as The Mennyms, *they appear in series such as* Bagpuss, Rosie and Jim *and* Ragdolly Anna.

Original rag dolls are becoming increasingly more valuable. At auction, collector's items can sell for thousands of pounds!

PUFFIN
WRITING
TIPS

Letters form a key part of the plotline in The Mennyms. *Write a letter every day, even if it's only a very short one! Think about who you're writing to and how the letter should be written.*

Ask a grown-up about their memories of childhood. You may discover a tale you've never come across before or hear something really inspiring and worth writing about!

Sylvia says, 'I remember the fun I had thinking of The Mennyms *as a "whodunnit" and deliberately planting clues. So here I offer you my fun activity questions.'*

What is the 'crime'?

Who is the guilty party?

What leads to the discovery of the truth?

Who makes this discovery?

(There are clues throughout the story that you can find!)

A Puffin Book can take you to amazing places.

WHERE WILL YOU GO?

#PackAPuffin

stories that last a **lifetime**

Ever wanted a friend who could take you to magical realms, talk to animals or help you survive a shipwreck? Well, you'll find them all in the **A PUFFIN BOOK** collection.

A PUFFIN BOOK will stay with you **forever**. Maybe you'll read it again and again, or perhaps years from now you'll suddenly **remember** the moment it made you **laugh** or **cry** or simply see things **differently**. Adventurers **big** and **small**, rebels out to **change** their world, even a mouse with a **dream** and a spider who can spell – these are the characters who make **stories** that last a **lifetime**.

Whether you love animal tales, war stories or want to know what it was like growing up in a different time and place, the **A PUFFIN BOOK** collection has a story for you – you just need to decide where you want to go next . . .